OBSESSIVE BOSS

WILLOW FOX

We've remodeled Club Sage, and I'm just about to burn the place down to the ground.

When Savannah comes looking for a job, I hire her on the spot. We're desperate for dancers, and she's stunning. How could she not be perfect for the job?

Don't mix business and pleasure—the advice I should have heeded from my mentor and boss, Nikita Krylova.

I let a federal agent into the workplace.

Savannah has access to the books and the money we launder.

I'm screwed if my boss Nikita or the head of the bratva, Mikhail, discovers my little indiscretion.

But they're bound to find out since Mikhail's better half, Madisyn, is former FBI. She worked with Savannah Blakely. Do I come clean and accept that I'm a dead man or bury the truth and a few bodies before anyone finds out?

ONE

SAVANNAH

I'm a virgin all over again, except this time, my first is being undercover. And it's not a little job. Supervisory Special Agent Barrett Kingston is sending me deep, to infiltrate the bratva.

And if that's not complicated enough, I have to make sure that I steer clear of Madisyn Carter, former FBI and a colleague of mine.

I'm a bundle of nervous energy wrapped in a neat little bow with a shy smile. I swallow down the anxiety and bury it as deep as I can because I can't screw this up.

The FBI higher-ups have demanded that we provide evidence against Mikhail Barinov and his crime organization. No easy task, but I'm not dealing with the Pakhan. My focus is on one of the men running the club. My mark is Anton Petrova.

I stroll up to Club Sage in a short black skirt and bright red top that matches my lipstick. It's not my usual attire, but I'm dressed to play the part and for my interview with Anton.

Yanking open the heavy door, I see that the club's interior is much darker than the outside, and it takes a moment for my eyes to adjust to the intense change.

"Can I help you?" a man with a thick Russian accent asks. He glances me up and down. It's not Anton. I've seen his picture enough times and memorized who I'm targeting to realize that this man is just another member of the bratva. The man at the door is nothing more than a glorified bodyguard.

"I have an interview," I say.

The place smells of fresh paint and wood. The interior is shiny, and the stage appears new. At first glance, the club has just opened, but the outside of the building shows its age. Something must have happened here to require such an extensive remodel.

There's no mention of it in the FBI or the newspapers. No report on the news signifying a remodel or the reason for one.

"Wait here," the man says. He tromps down the hall and out of view. A minute later, he returns. There's not an ounce of friendliness or warmth in his tone. "Follow me."

I oblige and accompany him down the long, dark hallway and then around the bar to the back. It's a small office, no windows and only one door.

"Hi, I'm Savannah," I say, introducing myself and handing him my resume.

"Thank you, Dmitri." The Russian who escorted me to the office shuts the door behind me on his way out. "I'm Anton." He drops the resume to the desk, uninterested in the paper and the information it contains.

I press my lips together. He hasn't gestured or told me to sit, so I stand opposite his desk, my hands folded in front of me.

"You dance?" Anton glances me over, his gaze scrutinizing every inch of my clothed skin.

"I've dabbled," I say. Agent Kingston insisted before this operation that I take a pole dancing class and train with an instructor. They weren't my finest hours, but I've improved quite a bit since the beginning. Enough that I should be able to pull off dancing. It's not like I'm fibbing that I've had years of experience.

"I need to see what you've got. Dance," Anton gestures at me and points to the small space in the room. He's not looking for a lap dance. He wants me to show him what I can do on my own.

My pulse quickens, and I place my purse on the nearby chair. I turn with my back to Anton and sway my hips, letting him stare at my ass while I work the top button on my red blouse free.

I spin around to face him, my shirt giving him a glimpse of my push-up bra, but I haven't shown all of it yet. I'll be wearing far less on stage, but he hasn't asked me to strip down. However, I'll probably be expected to do so during the interview, so I may as well give him a show.

The man isn't half bad-looking. Okay, if I'm to be blunt, Anton is hot. His dark brown eyes wander down my body. His hair is thick and dark. Dare say, I want to run my fingers through it. But I refrain.

He's in a buttoned-up suit, giving no indication of what's underneath his outfit. I'd like to undress him, rip his crisp white cotton shirt open and grab him by his tie, dragging him toward me and down onto his knees.

But I doubt that he'll let me dominate him.

He's the kind of man who exudes power and revels in being in control. Just imagining what it would be like in bed with him, makes my cheeks burn and helps me get into my role as a dancer for his club.

I use the small space and own it like I belong here because this can't fall apart if I want to climb my way up the bureau ladder.

The wooden desk sits between us, and I use it as a prop while dancing. I don't bother to ask for permission before climbing atop it, my platform heels allowing me to clomp against the wood. Thankfully, the room has tall ceilings.

Anton stares at me and leans back in his leather chair with a smug grin. I'm sure he can look up my skirt and see the thong I'm wearing. I expected that he'd require me to dance as part of the interview, and I wanted to be prepared.

I have to land this job. If he doesn't give it to me, I can't go sulking back to the FBI that I failed the most basic aspect of undercover work, getting in with the bad guys.

I sway my hips, and my hands smooth over my body, undoing the rest of the buttons on my blouse. I turn my back to Anton and slowly inch the shirt over my shoulders. My best moves are teasing and seductive. There's no pole in this office. I have to use what I know.

I run my fingers through my long blonde tresses and let my hand wander down across my bra as I let the red shirt fall to the floor. I won't wear a shirt and blouse when I dance for the club. I'll be in nothing more than a G-string and bikini top.

My black skirt wraps around my waist, and I dance and unclasp the clip holding the material together before letting it glide down to the floor.

Anton shifts in his seat and bites down on his bottom lip. The tips of his ears are bright red. Does he always get aroused by the entertainment? Or is it me?

The office door swings open without so much as a knock. Am I supposed to continue? As if there is music being played, I continue swaying and dancing.

Anton clears his throat and motions for me to get down. "I've seen enough."

"I'll chat with you after you're done," the gentleman who barged into the office says.

I recognize him from the background that I was forced to memorize. He's Nikita Krylova, one of Mikhail's men and the club's manager.

He retreats from the small office and shuts the door while I climb down from the desk and retrieve my clothes off the floor. I'm still in my matching scarlet panties and bra.

"The pay is shit. My other girls get priority on the main platform. You'll have to earn your place on the stage," Anton says. "The club takes fifty percent. You have to wear the clothes we provide and no sassing the patrons or giving any of the employees attitude. Also, no taking on private clients after hours. Are you still interested?"

"When do I start?" I ask.

TWO

ANTON

I'd been in my office all morning, interviewing, and only one girl showed up, a sexy blonde with the brightest blue eyes I've ever seen, Savannah Parker.

I would have hired her on the spot based on her looks and the set of tits and ass on the girl.

But I figured that I might as well make her dance, and boy, am I glad that I did. That was quite a show, and it was entirely for me.

Until my boss, Nikita, decided to burst right in without knocking. Couldn't he pretend to give a shit? The last thing I want is the new girl thinking that I'm below Nikita, even if he is my superior.

The man runs the club.

He doesn't own it. Mikhail, the head of the bratva, owns the business. But he's too busy with other matters to run every enterprise that he's involved himself in, which works out well for me. I get a portion of the proceeds brought in from the club, while Mikhail gets to launder money. It's a win-win for everyone.

I loosen my tie and stand. Savannah has already found her way out of the office. She has orders to return when we open this evening. Until then, she doesn't need to hang around. I don't need her discovering the shit we do around here.

I open the office door and head up the stairs for Nikita's private office. He's got a large office with an exceptional view that overlooks the dance floor with one-way glass. Even after the remodel, he kept the same floor plan and layout. His office is three times the size of mine. Although, in his defense, I spent quite a bit more time on the floor with the ladies and patrons.

Someone has to make sure the place is running smoothly, and although Nikita is the manager, I mingle with the guests, help when the floor is crowded with drink orders, and keep the place operating smoothly.

I ought to run the club, but I have no hard feelings for Nikita. We're brothers.

Unlike Nikita, who barges into my office, I knock before entering.

"It's open," Nikita says.

I step into his office and close the door behind myself.

He glances up from behind his desk, his pen poised in his hand, but he stops writing. "Cute girl you had in here earlier. Did you hire her?" Nikita asks.

"I did," I say and quirk a grin.

"Quite the dancer. Is that how you interview all your employees? Because I'd love to be part of the interview process."

"Shut up."

Nikita shrugs, not the least bit offended. "I'm taking off early tonight. I assume you can close for me."

He's not asking.

"You got it," I say. I shouldn't ask, but I can't stop myself from wanting to know if it's because of his new flame. "Do you have plans with Lucy?"

He's married, and while he doesn't strike me as a family man, the marriage was initially to protect Lucy and her son. But I think he's always harbored feelings for her, even when he hated her. Besides, the man can barely keep his claws off her.

"No, she's going shopping with Hannah."

"Better keep her on a tight leash," I joke.

"I'm not worried. Hannah is shopping for a wedding dress." Nikita flashes his wedding band at me. "The way I see it, I got off cheap."

"Careful, brother. Marrying her at the courthouse could come back to bite you in the ass. If she hears you talking like that, she'll be asking for a do-over wedding somewhere exotic and expensive."

While Nikita and I aren't blood brothers, we're both members of the bratva. We might as well be blood because our ties are just as strong.

"Don't go putting any ideas into her head," he warns.

"I wouldn't dream of it."

Nikita shuffles a few pages around on his desk. He glances up at me once more. "Did you run a background check on the new hire?"

"I did not." I wince at the realization that I was supposed to vet her qualifications before I offered the job. "Is that a problem? We're short two dancers." We're not down several more because Nikita paid them during renovations to ensure that when the club reopened, they would be ready to work.

Nikita glances at his watch as if that will indicate how long a background check will take.

Days.

We don't have days.

I'm down to a couple of hours and no more interviews for the afternoon. Besides, even if I had a half dozen girls lined up for the job, I wouldn't be able to run background on them, either.

"Just make sure her references check out. Did she strip at another club?" Nikita asks.

"I should probably look at her resume," I say, admitting that I hadn't even given it a cursory glance during the interview. I was too hung up on the cute blonde.

I clear my throat. I'm not usually this unprofessional when hiring dancers. Typically, I have more time between the interview and hiring them.

"You think?" Nikita is more than a bit snippy. "Begin the process on the background check, but we'll let her start work tonight."

———

I shouldn't be excited when Savannah enters the club. She's here to work, but my heart rate quickens.

Her eyes lock with mine, and she offers a shy smile. I don't fall for her innocent routine. She danced on my desk. The girl isn't the least bit shy.

Striding across the hall, I greet her for her first day. "Are you ready?" I ask as she follows me to the ladies' dressing room.

"I hope so," Savannah says with a nervous laugh. Her voice quivers, and I get the impression that she may not be used to dancing in front of men, but I gather that she'll like the attention. Most of the girls do, and those who don't quit.

On a metal rack are dozens of outfits for the girls to wear. "Anything on that rack, you can borrow. If you want to bring your clothes, you need clearance from management on every new outfit. Hair, makeup, and nails should be done before you get dressed. On the back wall, are heels you can borrow. Again, anything that you want to bring needs to be cleared by Nikita or myself."

"No boots," another girl says as she sits in front of a mirror, applying her liquid eyeliner. "And you pick your wardrobe last."

"Bailey, you give a warm welcome," I mutter at her.

"I've got seniority," Bailey says.

"And you bring ninety percent of your clothes. I don't know why you feel it necessary to harass the new kid."

"I'm not some kid," Savannah quips. "I can take care of myself."

I'm surprised by the new girl's boldness. "Fine, by all means." I shut the door, leaving the girls on their own before the stage show begins.

I need to keep my distance.

Savannah is off-limits. She's a dancer, and I'm management. This thing between us, the spark, has to be extinguished.

I clear my throat, stalk away from the girls' dressing room, and knock into Nikita.

"You're in a rush," he grunts, glancing me over. His eyes tighten, and he grabs my arm, dragging me into one of the back storage rooms where we house our liquor.

"What?" I don't know why he's found it necessary to drag me away from the floor. I haven't done anything wrong yet.

"I've seen that look," Nikita says. "I wore it for weeks while dealing with Lucy."

I clear my throat. "Is that before or after you married her?" I honestly don't know what look he's talking about, but I'm trying to steer the conversation far from the new hire.

"Before, when she made me so angry, all I wanted was to bend her over and have my way with her."

I choose my words carefully. "Yeah, I've seen the way you look at her." Anyone would be blind to miss the heated stares they exchanged, even when they swore they hated one another.

"Trust me when I say you stare at the new girl the same way."

"She's just a dancer. I interview all my dancers in the same manner. She's nothing special." I nearly have to choke the words out because even I don't believe them.

Savannah shouldn't be special; she's just another girl we've hired to entertain the guests.

But there's something about her that I can't quite let go of, maybe the fact I'd like a private dance or two and a session alone with her in a suite.

"Tonight, go out for drinks. Get whatever the hell it is out of your system because you need to be focused on work. And then come back tomorrow and be your grumpy, asinine self."

"I have to cover the club tonight. Are you offering to take my shift?"

"No, but you need to find a hot piece of ass and forget about the new girl."

I snort under my breath. In what spare time? He makes it sound easy, and getting girls isn't hard for me, but I don't need my one-night stands showing up where I work. I prefer to keep my private life separate from my job. "I'll get right on that, boss."

I head to my office and crack the seal on the vodka, pouring myself a drink.

What does Nikita know?

Savannah is just another girl, a dancer. She's nothing to me. Sure, she's gorgeous with that long blonde hair and those bright baby-blue eyes, but I'm all about personality, not looks.

I down another shot of vodka, attempting to convince myself that I feel nothing for her.

Nikita has gotten under my skin.

I huff out of my office and onto the main floor. A few customers are seated, sipping their drinks, and watching Bailey on stage.

Savannah hasn't emerged from the dressing room yet, but she has ten more minutes until she's late.

I wander the main floor, keeping an eye on the guests. Since the run-in with the Italians a couple of months ago, we have added security measures. Otello and several of his buddies came in, guns blazing.

Gunfire erupts from all around. Men in suits cover the entrance and exit. They don't bother with masks. They want us to know who they are, and a message will be delivered.

"Where's Nikita?" Otello asks in his thick Italian accent. The man wreaks of vodka like he bathes in it or wears it as a cologne.

He shoves a gun under my chin as two men blast the place with bullets. "Upstairs," I say. I don't flinch or cower. I want to warn Nikita and his new flame that trouble is coming, but there isn't time.

"Best you run home and warn the family our fight isn't over," Otello says. He lowers his gun but doesn't shoot me. He has the opportunity. They could kill the dancers or the patrons, but they've let them flee out the side exit like they want them shuttling out that door while they stand guard, blasting the walls and tables, the bar and stage with bullets. Shrapnel flies in every direction, slicing my arm.

I heed Otello's warning. I get out while I still can, breathing, and my heart is beating. The Italians aren't known for their kindness or for letting men live, especially their enemies.

The parking lot is fraught with screams and fear. A fury of panic, as people jump into their vehicles and blare their horns, trying to cut each other off. Everyone wants to get away as quickly as possible.

I grab my keys from my pocket. My phone is in my office. I'm not going back for it. I jump into my vehicle, start the engine, and pull out of the parking lot. I head straight for the compound. I need to see Mikhail, the Pakhan, and tell him what the hell is going on at the club. They'll want to send reinforcements and backup, assuming it's not too late.

The building stills smells of fresh paint. The wood floors have been refinished and the interior redesigned and remodeled. But my nostrils tingle with the smell of gunpowder, and a chill runs down my spine, while there is no imminent danger tonight.

The additional guards at all entrances and exits keep the building secure. We have a new surveillance system that records everything on-site and sends a copy to the cloud for storage. Behind the bar, is a silent alarm that notifies the compound and Mikhail's men if anything happens.

Next time, we'll be prepared. But I hope there isn't a next time, that the war between the Italians and Russians is over for good.

Savannah struts out of the dressing room in a pair of silver lace-up pumps. They sparkle and match the sexy little outfit that she's wearing.

Is that one of our outfits? I can't recall a girl wearing it before, at least not as well as Savannah. That girl is a fucking goddess.

Her hair is tied back, and she doesn't glance at me as she stalks her way onto the floor and steps onto the smaller platform. Bailey or one of the other girls must have told her where she was positioned on stage.

We're not solely a strip club. If we were, it would be against the law. There's a 60/40 rule that any adult business must devote no more than 40% of its square footage to adult entertainment. We bend the rules. Greasing the right men helps them turn a blind eye. Mikhail had discussed making changes during the renovations, but it was decided to keep the same layout. Guests like to feel at home, and we have repeat clientele who choose our establishment over others.

Her platforms click over the wooden floorboards, and even with the pulse-pounding music, I swear I can hear and feel the beat of her shoes over the floor. She climbs onto the small stage and begins her dance.

I want to watch, mesmerized by everything about her. I stare at her a little too long, and she glances at me, offering a coy smile. She's a vixen. There's no way she's shy or new at dancing. The woman owns the stage by how her hips sway and she grabs hold of the pole. She's outshining the regular girls, who are used to the constant onslaught of attention from the patrons.

They're going to hate her. She's not playing fair or sharing attention. Though it's not her fault she's new, the men like fresh meat. And even though we're reopening now, she's still new blood on the dance floor. Our patrons tend to be regulars, and while they might have been frequenting other establishments until we reopened, one look at Savannah and I swear they're as hooked as I am.

I head in the opposite direction, for my office. I swear I need a cold shower and a stiff drink—a distraction.

I bide my time for most of the night in my office. I should be on the floor, greeting guests and ensuring everyone is happy. But I've heard no complaints, and I'm sure someone working the floor will find me if it is necessary.

"Come in," I say. If it were Nikita, he'd have barged in without thinking twice.

Savannah stands at the door. She's no longer in her silvery sequin attire, making it easier for me to look at her without my jaw hitting the floor. "What can I do for you?" I ask, placing my pen down on the desk.

"I'm new to the area," Savannah says. "I was hoping you might recommend someplace I could grab a late bite to eat?"

"At this hour?" I glance at my watch and stand. "Are any of the other girls accompanying you?" I don't like the thought of her wandering the streets of New York after two in the morning.

"I doubt it," she says and glances down at her feet.

Standing, I grab my suit coat off the back of my chair and slide it over my shoulders. "I'll go with you," I say.

"You don't have to do that—"

"I don't have to, but I am," I say. I shut off the lights in the office and lock the door. My hand falls to her lower back as I accompany her down the hallway and toward the back exit.

The club is closed for the night. The girls are heading out to their cars. Dmitri is the last to leave, with orders to lock up the place after I hit the road.

"Did you drive here?" I ask as we head out into the parking lot. I only take note of Dmitri's vehicle and my own. The other spaces are empty. The girls had just piled out together in unison. Savannah should be trying to befriend them, not the boss.

"I don't have a car," Savannah says.

"How do you get around town?"

"Subway, same as everyone else." She points in the direction of the station.

"It's fourteen blocks. You aren't walking to the subway." She's lucky the train runs all night, the perk of being a New Yorker. The city doesn't sleep. I hit the button to unlock the doors on my SUV. "Get in."

She sighs and relents, climbing into the front passenger seat. "Thanks. You can just drop me off at the station."

"I thought you were hungry."

"Well, I am," she stammers, pulling the seatbelt low and tight across her lap, "b-but I don't want to put you out."

"I could use a bite," I say. No one will care if I arrive back at the compound early in the morning. I'm used to late nights.

I pull out of the parking lot. Traffic is light, and there's hardly anyone on the road at this hour, making it easy to navigate across town to one of the best cafés open 24/7.

"How long have you managed the club?" Savannah asks.

"Since practically forever," I say. I don't go into specifics with her. It's none of her damn business when I began helping with the club; technically, Nikita is management. I'm beneath him but handle the dancers and all the new hires.

"What about you? What'd you do before dancing?" I ask. I wince, realizing the giveaway that I didn't, in fact, read her resume. But what would a piece of paper tell me that I couldn't get from the interviewee?

"I went to college for accounting," Savannah says. She stares ahead at the road before briefly glancing in my direction.

"Did you finish?" I can't imagine that she did and decided to apply as a dancer unless she's in debt and strictly looking to make a lot of money fast.

"Freshman year, I bombed out for too much partying." Savannah chuckles and glances down. Her left-hand plays with her hair, curling a strand around her finger. Is that a nervous habit that she's picked up?

"I'll bet your parents weren't too happy."

"They were not pleased and cut me off. They told me to get a job and support myself. Which is what I did."

She quirks an awkward smile and glances in my direction.

I understand there's more to the story she's not sharing, but I don't push. It's none of my business, as long as she doesn't get in trouble.

"How long have you been out of college?" I ask and clear my throat. The girl is over twenty-one. I had made a copy of her driver's license with her new hire paperwork, but I can't quite remember her date of birth. I skimmed over the information at the time.

"Quite a few years," Savannah says. "I've dabbled with jobs but haven't found my footing. I guess you can say I'm a bit of a free spirit. Which is what led me to dance."

"A free spirit that wanted to get a degree in accounting?"

She chuckles and glances down at her lap. I pull into the parking lot of the café and shut off the engine. "I never said the accounting degree was my idea. But I do have a knack for numbers."

"Let me guess. You're a bit of a rebel, and your parents were the ones who wanted you to go to college for accounting?"

"My father," Savannah says and crinkles her nose. "Enough about him." She opens the vehicle door, and I do the same, climbing out.

The morning air is fresh and cool, clean. The moon is nearly full, and even though the city lights detract from the starry night sky, the darkness is welcoming.

I open the door to the café, escorting her inside and to a table at the back. On my way to the booth, I grab two menus, making myself right at home. We own the café, not that I intend to tell Savannah about our business dealings.

"We don't have to wait for the hostess?" Savannah asks as she glances behind her. Eventually, she follows me to the table and sits across from me.

"Not at this hour," I say, handing her a menu. My back is to the wall, and my gaze is on the front entrance. I never like to keep my back at any door. I need to be always alert and aware of my surroundings.

She slumps down into the booth, grabs her menu, and gives it a cursory glance. "What do you recommend?" she asks. Unlike at the club, where she was wearing practically nothing, her blue jeans and baggy sweatshirt make her adorable.

Her roughness makes her a million times more charming than the fancy rich girl persona I've seen the dancers portray. Although I doubt any girls were wealthy before dancing, they like to act as though they live a lavish lifestyle. Maybe some of them do. I don't keep tabs on them at home.

"Any suggestions?" she asks again.

"Everything is delicious." I can't speak an ill word about this place. Even if we didn't own it, the food is fantastic.

"That helps to narrow it down." There's a smile on the blonde's face; it's genuine, and her shoulders relax, like she's finally able to wind down.

"Did you enjoy your first night?" I ask.

I put the menu down. I don't need to look at it. I've memorized it in its entirety. But it was a nice, welcoming distraction when I needed a break from making conversation. For some reason, I don't feel the least bit awkward with Savannah.

Maybe a mix of passion and chemistry is swirling in the air, making it impossible to stop staring at her.

She twirls her hair again around her finger, and this time her bottom lip tugs between her teeth as she stares down at the menu, examining it. "Will you order for me? I need to use the ladies' room."

"Any allergies?" I ask. I don't know what she likes, but I know what I want, and it's not solely the food I'm after.

I clear my throat, needing to rid my thoughts of Savannah dancing.

"Nope," she says. She grabs her clutch and carries it to the bathroom, wandering around for a moment, precariously lost, before finding the right way to the ladies' room.

Pulling my phone from my jacket pocket, I glance at the screen. Nothing urgent. Most of Mikhail's men are asleep at this hour, minus a handful of guards and security keeping the compound safe.

The waitress comes over while Savannah is in the bathroom, and I order for both of us. I'm tempted to have the waitress bring us a bottle of wine. Liquor isn't served here, but we always have a half dozen bottles in the back for when we bring guests in on business.

Not that this is business.

It's Savannah.

She's a dancer. Does this make the engagement pleasure? I shift uncomfortably with the mere suggestion. The girl does have a rocking body, and after seeing her performance in my office, it's hard not to imagine her legs wrapped around a pole.

I did everything in my power not to watch her dance tonight, practically locking myself in my office.

Maybe I should fire her. At least if she's not working at the club, she's not a distraction. I pinch the bridge of my nose. I can't fire her because she's hot. She's a dancer, for fuck's sake! She's supposed to be gorgeous.

Savannah struts back to the booth, her clutch at her side. Her fingernails are painted a dark red. I swear the color is *Sinful Seduction* or some other type of name that describes Savannah as much as the luscious red color.

She slides back into the booth across from me. The waitress brings us both a glass of water. I'd prefer something stronger, but I'm trying to remain in control and not let my dick make all the moves.

"Have you seen the bathrooms in this place?" Savannah asks.

I raise an inquisitive eyebrow, waiting for her to elaborate.

"The stalls are bigger than the bathroom in my apartment."

She brings a laugh right out of me. "New York isn't a cheap city to live in," I say.

"Tell me about it," she mutters under her breath.

"Roommates?" I ask. I can't imagine she's got her own place, although I hope she does because if there's any chance of me ever taking her home, I'd hate to run into anyone else who lives with her.

"Just me." Savannah shakes her head. "I used to live above a bar, making sleeping difficult until after two in the morning."

"And that's why you chose to dance?" I doubt that's the reason. She doesn't strike me as a girl who goes to bed early, but I could be wrong.

"No." She smiles, and her hand goes up to her hair, twirling the wayward strand again. "I don't have the money to attend bartending school, and I've tried waiting tables. I am clumsy, and the tips are terrible when you're dropping food and drinks on everyone's lap."

I cover my mouth with my hand to keep the laugh within my belly from seeping out. "Sorry," I apologize because I'm wearing the biggest grin, and she groans in agony. "I'm glad Nikita didn't convince me to hire you as a waitress."

"Nikita?"

"He's the manager of Club Sage. You met him during your interview," I say, reminding her of our little interruption.

"Right." She nods and pauses as she remembers him. "I didn't see him tonight at the club."

"He had plans tonight, but generally, he works the evening shift. I always work until close." Now that Nikita is a family man, he has less desire to work until two in the morning. I don't blame him. Lucy is quite adorable. Unsurprisingly, he'd want to crawl into bed with her before the sun rises.

"That's good to know." Savannah quirks a grin. "Listen, I hope I didn't come off during the interview as a little too forward, dancing on your desk and all that." She laughs and covers her face with her hand. She's embarrassed about the situation.

"You did great. It made me hire you on the spot," I say. Just thinking about her moves, her body, and how she stared at me, makes my pulse pound and stirs me up inside.

I reach for my glass of water, my mouth parched. The girl makes me hot, even when she's not trying to turn me on.

She's locked onto my gaze. "Okay, good. I don't normally dance on desks during interviews."

I choke on my water and cough, reaching for my napkin. "I hope not, especially if you're interviewing as a waitress. Do you plan on getting a second job?" I hate to think she might need to work somewhere else than the club.

Savannah smiles and closes her mouth, tight-lipped. She shakes her head. "I made more tonight than I've made in quite a while. As long as the girls don't kill me for stealing some of their regulars, I think I'm good."

"I can talk with Bailey and the other girls," I say. If anyone is giving her a hard time, it's Bailey. The girl has a mouth on her, but I doubt she'd throw a punch in an actual fight.

"Please don't do that. I don't want to alienate any of the girls. I want them to see that I'm not a threat, and having the boss show special treatment isn't going to help me."

She's right. I exhale a breath and nod. "Fair enough."

The waitress brings over fresh rolls and several dishes.

"Everything smells wonderful," she says.

"It tastes even better."

———

After a very late dinner, if you can even call it that, I handle the bill and escort Savannah to my vehicle. "What's your address?"

"You can drop me off at the train station," she says.

"No, I'm driving you home." I won't let her walk alone at four in the morning, wandering the streets. It's dangerous, especially for a pretty girl.

"You don't have to—"

"Address." I'm firm and curt, awaiting her answer.

She gives me the address of her place, and I tap the screen on my phone, inputting the information into GPS. I know the city rather well, but it's best to ensure I don't miss the building.

"Thanks." She slinks beside me, fastens her seatbelt, and glances out the window. I'd expect her to be tired, but she's as wide awake as I am.

The drive is quiet. I half-wonder if we've run out of conversation, and then she interrupts the silence.

"You're the first boss I've ever had who was nice to me," Savannah says. Her voice is barely above a whisper, but she intends for me to hear her.

I glance at her as I pull up near her apartment and parallel park outside. "Now, don't go telling the other girls I'm a nice guy. That'll ruin my reputation," I joke.

She smiles and unfastens her seatbelt as I put the vehicle into park. "Do you want to come in for a nightcap?"

I doubt she's asking about drinks, but this line, once it's crossed, I can't walk away and pretend it didn't happen.

It's a bad idea. The absolute worst, sleeping with one of the dancers. But she's only invited me in for a drink. She hasn't asked me to her bedroom or to undress.

I shut off the engine and climb out. At the very least, I should ensure that she gets into her apartment without issue. It's late. A few men are wandering the streets, although I haven't seen any in front of her door. Even so, anyone could be in the hallways waiting to attack a pretty young girl like Savannah.

I need to walk her to her door.

I don't answer her question, but I follow her inside the building, up the stairs to the fifth floor. It's a good thing that I'm in shape, or I'd be winded. Savannah is light on her feet, but I can hear her breathing catch up to her on the last flight of stairs.

"Quite a workout, right?" she asks, keeping her voice down, but it echoes in the stairwell. She opens the door to the fifth floor, and I follow, glancing down the long, dark hallway, making sure no one is loitering.

Savannah retrieves her house key from the clutch in her hand and fiddles with it before sliding it into the lock.

I stand outside her doorway for a second longer than necessary.

She glances over her shoulder, perhaps sensing my hesitation. "Do you want a drink?"

Wordlessly, I enter and shut the door, locking it behind myself. I shouldn't want a drink. I shouldn't want to be intoxicated around her, but all I want to do is rip her clothes off and drive my cock, burying it deep inside her warmth.

"A drink would be good. I'll have whatever you're having," I say.

Just one drink.

Then, I'll go home, back to the compound where my secrets stay locked up nice and tight.

Savannah disappears into the kitchen, and I shrug out of my jacket, leaving it on the dining room chair. I loosen my tie. I don't want to make myself at home, but I'm also ready to unwind, and maybe a drink will do just that.

She returns to the living room carrying two shot glasses and a bottle of rum. "Sorry, it's probably a bit girly for your tastes, but it's all I have in the cabinet." She sits on the floor, placing the shot glasses on the coffee table.

I follow her lead, accompanying her on the carpet. It's plush and feels considerably new. "It's fine," I say and read the label on the bottle. "*Passionfruit rum.* Very girly."

She hogs the bottle, holding it to her chest with one hand. "Would you prefer water?"

"No, pour me a shot." I'm not trying to complain, just stating the facts.

She smiles and hands me the bottle. I pour both of us a shot and place the rum bottle on the table. I don't bother to screw the lid back on. She didn't invite me in for one drink, did she?

THREE

SAVANNAH

I've barely been in the apartment a week, setting up for the undercover operation. Hopefully, the place looks lived in, and Anton doesn't suspect anything. The landlord provided us with a fresh apartment with new paint and carpet. The scent still tickles my nose when I waltz through the front door.

But Anton hasn't mentioned it; maybe he isn't as sensitive to the chemical smells.

I grab the shot glass and lift it. "To new opportunities," I say.

Anton lifts his glass and clinks mine with a nod before we both swallow back the shot.

Unlike when Madisyn went undercover with the bratva, there are no cameras or video surveillance inside my apartment. No audio bugs, as far as I'm aware. The place is immaculate, and I insisted it had to be that way.

My boss is turning a blind eye to the fact that I intend to sleep with Anton to gain his trust, and in doing that, I don't want it recorded for anyone at the bureau to witness.

I'm a bit wild, but I'm not that kinky. Sex tapes, I'm all for, but not having the videos paraded around the office for anyone to view as part of the evidence in a takedown of the bratva. No, thanks.

I intentionally brush against Anton's left hand as I reach for the bottle of rum and pour another round. "No wife or girlfriend at home?" I ask, glancing at his bare hand.

He offers a sly smile. "I've always put my work first. That doesn't tend to sit well for many people." He downs the shot, and I pour him another before taking my second.

I shift around the table, not the least bothered by his remark, and he takes the third shot of rum like a pro.

"I'm not like most girls," I say, pinning him with my stare.

Anton clears his throat and runs a hand through his hair. His eyes tighten, and I can sense his hesitation. For a bad guy, he doesn't seem that terrible of a man. He hasn't forced himself on me. Hell, the man hasn't even tried to kiss me. I thought when I invited him into my place, he'd have taken the bait and made the first move.

I grab him by his tie and pull him closer and tighter against me. In my most sultry voice, I whisper, "I can't stop thinking about when we first met and I danced on your desk."

It was only a few hours ago, but I wanted him to know that he stirred a desire deep within me. I climb onto his lap, straddling him.

Anton lets out a breathy sigh, and before he can object, I plant my lips firmly on his. My fingers tangle in his thick dark locks. He tastes like rum and spice. His masculine scent tickles my nose and stirs my insides.

With Anton, I don't have to pretend to be attracted to him. It's real, even if my life and who I say that I am is a lie.

He takes the gesture as motivation, and his kisses are both strong and forceful, unrelenting. He nips on my bottom lip, tugging it between his teeth, and I swear the man growls at me.

It's predatory.

Sexual.

And I'm about to come undone by the sounds the man makes. Fuck, I'm supposed to be the one in control.

But somehow, he takes the lead and lifts me into his arms. My legs wrap around his waist. Our mouths seem practically fused, unable to tear apart long enough to breathe.

I need him to trust me, fall for me, and let me into his inner circle, and sex is the easiest way to gain his trust.

He stumbles toward the bedroom. Considering the apartment is small, and he traps me between the door to the bedroom, with my back pressed flush against the wood, it's not hard to find.

"Open it." His word is a command. My hands grapple at the door handle before clinging to him again, dragging his shirt up and over his head. Except it gets stuck. "Buttons," he mutters, and if I was trying to disorient him, I do a damn good job as he grumbles under his breath.

I slide down his body, my feet firmly landing on the floor. My back is to the mattress, but I feel it against my legs, and I could lie down. But I don't, not yet.

Instead, I reach around to help Anton with the buttons when he rips the shirt free and clear from his chest, tossing it across the room.

"Undress and get on the bed," he growls at me. I take a sharp breath and cross my arms at my hips, lifting my sweatshirt over my head. I'm not even wearing a bra underneath. "Pants, too," he orders.

I unbutton and unzip my jeans, slowly sliding them down my hips. I leave my panties and scoot back onto the mattress, crawling back to the pillows as he stalks me like I'm his prey.

He's not the least bit gentle or slow as he devours my lips. Anton is rough, but it's perfect as he straddles my waist and pins my arms down against the mattress.

"I've been wanting to taste you since you came into my office," he rasps, and my heart quickens at his admission.

I'd seen the desire behind his darkened gaze, much like it is now, his attention devoted entirely to me.

"Roll over," he whispers into my ear, and I can't help but wonder what he has in mind.

When I don't follow his command quickly enough, he releases his grip on my arms, and I inhale sharply, afraid that he will walk away.

But he doesn't. Instead, his hands tease my hips, flipping me around, and he guides my ass into the air. "I want you on all fours," he whispers, patting my bottom, his hand lingering over the lacy panties I wore just for him.

I hear him shucking his clothes to the floor, boxers and all. I glance at him over my shoulder, wanting to see him naked. He isn't just an assignment. Maybe that's all he should be—he's bratva, and I'm a federal agent. But I haven't had sex in too many months, and Anton is more than just a man with a pulse. Although, if I'm to be honest, that helps.

He's hot, making me even more eager to do this with him.

"Are you going to fuck me?" I ask. I'm already breathless and antsy. My insides throb and pulsate.

"You'd like that, *kitten*, wouldn't you?" he smirks.

I would, but he's taking his damn ass time. He bends down to pick up his suit and fold his slacks. Is he trying to kill me? Maybe he knows I'm a federal agent; this is just a game to him.

I shift to turn around and sit on my ass since he hasn't returned to the bed, when I feel his hand smack my bottom.

"Oww!" I squeal, and my eyes widen in horror. "What the hell was that for?" Did he seriously just spank me? A grown woman.

He puts me back in the position that he wants me, on all fours. His body touches mine from behind. I glance back over my shoulder at his thick cock, and I gasp at the sight. My mouth is dry, and I have the urge to lick my lips. Already, my insides ache, and it's going to hurt a hell of a lot more than just a little pinch.

He's large.

Huge.

And I want his cock buried deep inside of me, but I'm also terrified. He's a man not to be messed with, a member of the bratva, who will kill for his brothers, and when he finds out I betrayed him, I'll be his next target.

He can never find out.

Well, maybe never is a bit of an overstatement. I have to take whatever evidence I find and turn it in to my superiors. But damn, my gaze is locked on Anton's cock, and it twitches as he tears the foil packet with his teeth.

I shut my eyes and revel in the warmth of his touch and the excitement that tingles throughout my entire body.

His digits are warm and inviting as he separates my folds and eases his cock inside me.

I gasp and grip the bedsheets with my fists, hanging my head. The pain is almost unbearable, but it's good. Riveting and unyielding, he grabs my hips and thrusts into my tightness. He stretches me to accommodate his size. My brain is foggy, my mind going as my body takes over and I let him have his way with me.

Anton grunts, and he's not the least bit quiet or silent. I love the sounds coming from his throat, his mouth, and the gasps that he makes as I tighten onto his cock with each thrust.

"Woman, you're going to kill me," he whispers.

And I quirk a wicked grin. "Good," I shoot back at him, glancing over my shoulder.

His eyes are heavy and dark. He's struggling to hold on and make the moment last. He's not the only one. I need to gain his trust and his confidence. I can't make this into a one-night stand where I'm nothing more than a mistake he made.

"Are you close?"

My insides pulsate, but I've never particularly had orgasms from sex. I whimper unintentionally, and I swear it's like the man reads my mind.

One hand moves from my hip to my nightstand, and I'm mortified that I hadn't realized it sooner. I had left my vibrator out for him to see. That hadn't been on purpose.

He flips the switch on the side and hands the vibrator to me. "You come when I tell you," Anton commands.

I nod, eagerly obeying him when he hands me the vibrator. The motor's hum makes my voice catch because I know what's coming, and I'm already close. I'm just not quite there with him yet.

I press the head of the vibrator against my clit as Anton pounds into me. My mouth parts, and I gasp, the moans spilling past my lips as I struggle to keep myself on all fours.

"Not yet, baby girl," he rasps, and I whimper in protest.

"Please," I'm not above begging. My insides pulsate, and the thrum of the vibrator pressed tight against my swollen bead brings a warmth spreading across my body, a riveting heat that can't be undone.

My insides tighten and pulsate. "Come for me, baby girl," he whispers. I swear it comes out more like a growl, a command I eagerly obey.

The orgasm stretches through me as my toes curl. I clench onto his cock, and my hand tightens on the shaft of the purple vibrator.

Anton is right with me, grunting, his breathing deepening and intensifying as he lets go. A moment later, he withdraws and removes the condom, finding his way into the bathroom.

I shut off the vibrator and leave it on the bedside table. There's no point in hiding it. Collapsing onto the mattress, my heart pounds against my chest as I attempt to catch my breath.

Anton steps out of the bathroom and glances at his clothes like he's deciding if he should go.

I'm exhausted and sated, but I crawl onto all fours. He steps toward the bed, his fingers combing through my hair, dragging my chin up toward his. Inadvertently, I purr. I don't know where the sound comes from. I swear I've never made it before from my own throat.

"You're mine, *kitten*," he growls and captures my mouth with another searing kiss before guiding me onto my back.

"Stay the night," I whisper between kisses.

"It's almost morning."

The sun hasn't come up yet, but it will soon. "Stay for breakfast?" I yawn and shuffle under the covers, patting the bed beside me.

His gaze tightens. "For a little bit."

I don't know what he's thinking, but he slips under the covers and pulls me against him. He's warm and strong. His masculine scent tickles my nose as my back is to him. His arms surround me, and for a man insisting that he's only staying a little while, I get the impression that's not what he wants, with his body cocooned around mine.

───────

After several hours of blissful slumber, my arm reaches out to the cold mattress beside me.

Damn.

I sigh heavily and force my eyes to glance at the digital projection clock. It's practically the afternoon.

It's time I get my ass out of bed and start the day. I grumble under my breath and sit up in bed when I smell the faint aroma of coffee.

"Anton?" I climb out of bed and grab a t-shirt from my dresser and a pair of panties, slipping them on before stepping out of the bedroom.

"Coffee is ready," Anton says like he lives here and owns the place. "Do you want me to pour you a cup?"

I pinch the bridge of my nose. "Uh, yeah, that would be great." I have a bit of a headache, although I'm not sure why. Probably because I'm not used to such late hours. I will have to get used to it, working at the club.

The coffee mugs on the wall make it easy for him to find and grab one for me. He already has a steaming cup on the kitchen counter for himself.

I stumble into the kitchen and open the fridge, grabbing a carton of oat milk creamer. I add a dash after he fills my cup with coffee. "Thanks," I say.

"How'd you sleep?" he asks.

I lift the mug and inhale the aroma before taking a sip. It's hot, but the creamer helps cool the coffee enough that I won't burn my tongue or the roof of my mouth. "Good. You?"

I'm relieved that he's still here, and while it'd be good for him to be gone so that I can head out and report to the FBI that my mission is going well, I like that he hasn't run off.

"I got a few hours of sleep." He brings the mug to his lips and takes a sip. He's already dressed, and I suspect he'd have left if I hadn't gotten up.

"You're dressed," I say and glance behind me toward the bathroom. "I thought we maybe could shower together this morning."

"I would love that, *kitten*, but I have to meet up with my boss in an hour."

"A fast shower?"

"Nothing with you is fast," he growls and steps closer. He places his mug on the counter and wraps his arms around my waist, pulling me tight against him. He nibbles on my bottom lip, one hand rakes through my hair, and the other remains planted on my hip.

Anton's cell phone buzzes in his pocket. "Sorry," he apologizes and releases his tight hold, stepping into the living room to take the call. There's not much privacy, but he's keeping me from hearing whatever is being said on the other end of the call.

"Hey, Nikita, what's up?"

I sip my coffee, pretending not to be interested, listening to one side of the conversation.

"You don't have anyone else who can do it?" Anton emits a heavy sigh.

The floor plan leaves the kitchen open to the living room, so while he's trying to have some privacy, his demeanor indicates that he's stressed.

"Text me the address." Anton runs a hand through his hair and emits a heavy sigh as he ends the call.

"I have to go," he says, striding back into the kitchen.

"Is everything okay?"

"Just work stuff," he says, not indicating what's happening. He shoves his cell phone back into his interior suit pocket. "We need to keep this a secret if you want it to continue."

"I do," I say with a firm nod and eager smile. "That's probably for the best. I don't want the other girls to get jealous or think that's why I landed the job."

Anton leans in and presses his lips against mine before heading out the door. "I'll see you tonight at the club."

I didn't have time to place a tracker on his vehicle and a bug inside. And I can't do it while we're at the club. There is too much surveillance outside and potential witnesses who work for the bratva. I'll have to try again tonight after work. Hopefully, I can steal another night with him and plant the devices without being seen.

FOUR

ANTON

I can't believe Nikita wants me to pick up his kid, Zion, from school. Technically, it's Lucy's son, but they're married, and he treats the kid as if he's his flesh and blood. I'm not saying it's bad, but bringing your employee into it by asking him to get the kid from elementary school isn't the least bit ordinary.

Although, when is anything we do typical?

I hate leaving Savannah without at least discussing what happened last night. She caught me off guard, and I swear I didn't plan on fucking her.

But I'm glad that I did.

Nikita would have a fit if he found out, and I don't even want to see Mikhail's reaction. I'd probably be reprimanded, and Savannah would be fired.

I can't let that happen to her. She doesn't deserve to lose her job because I can't stop thinking about her naked. And now, having seen her naked, a part of me doesn't want to let her back on stage for the other men to ogle her while she dances.

But it's her job, and I've never been particularly jealous. Of course, I also hadn't slept with any dancers or employees until last night. Well, technically, this morning.

I head down to the vehicle and climb into the SUV. The vehicle isn't mine. The bratva owns it, along with a dozen or so other cars loaned amongst us.

Pulling out my phone, I open the most recent text message from Nikita and click on the address, opening the GPS on my phone. I'm familiar with the city but don't particularly pay attention to the school the kid goes to or where it's located. It's not any of my business until now.

I can't believe he has me running errands for him, but in his defense, his wife, Lucy, tripped down the stairs at home and needs her right foot examined at the hospital. The girl is clumsy.

Nikita would never lay a hand on her; while she's in the compound, she's safe. My phone would have lit up if something happened, like a break-in. Undoubtedly, one of several associates would have reached out to warn me of the attack.

I swing by the elementary school and park the vehicle in line, stepping out and standing near the SUV. I swear all the kids look the same from a distance with their backpacks slung over their shoulders. It doesn't help that the kids all wear the same school uniform.

Since when did Nikita foot the bill for a private school?

It's none of my business, but neither is picking up Zion from school, and here I am, running errands for the boss. I glance at my watch, and the kid comes skipping over to me. "Hi, Uncle Anton."

I'm technically not the kid's uncle, but that's how he's been taught to address us in public. "Are you ready to go?" I ask.

His teacher hurries after him, a short older woman with graying hair. At least, I assume it's his teacher. Maybe she's the principal? "Mr. Petrova," she calls out to me as she approaches.

"Yes."

"I need you to sign Anton out before taking him home. Can you show me some identification?"

My jaw tightens, but it's not like my identification is a secret. "Sure," I say, pulling my wallet out from my back pocket and opening it, revealing my driver's license. I don't bother taking it out of the plastic. The woman can read through a clear piece of plastic, right?

"Thank you. If you can, just sign this," she says, shoving the clipboard at my chest.

I scribble my name on the sheet of paper before she hurries off to accost the next parent or guardian. I open the back door and nod for Zion to climb in. When he doesn't budge, I raise an inquisitive eyebrow. "Get in."

"There's no booster seat," he says. "Mom says I can't go in the car without one."

"Well, kid, your mom isn't here."

Zion's bottom lip pouts. Is he about to cry? Because I can't handle a crying seven-year-old. Some days, I can barely look after myself.

"How about we grab ice cream on the way home?" I suggest, trying to think of a reason to keep the kid from bawling. If he has a meltdown, I don't know how I'll handle it. Picking the kid up and tossing him into the backseat, while tempting, would bring too much attention. The kid isn't going to be silent.

Zion exhales a heavy sigh and relents, climbing into the backseat. "Fine." He drops his bookbag on the floor beside his feet.

I swear he has his mother's attitude, not that I've worked with Lucy that much. She danced one night at the club, and Nikita made it clear that would never happen again. Too bad; she was a cute dancer. She was nowhere near as sexy as Savannah, but she had a few spicy moves. She bartends a couple of nights a week when we need the extra coverage.

After Zion is situated in the middle seat and buckles in, I slam the door shut and hurry around to the driver's side.

"Mom is going to kill you," Zion says as he tips his head back and stares up at the ceiling.

What the hell is so interesting up there?

"Why is that?" I'm not sure why I even bother to ask, but I do.

He ticks each item off on his fingers. "No booster seat and giving me ice cream after school. You're so dead," Zion says with a chuckle.

"That's only two reasons."

"Do you want more?"

Gosh, the kid is snippy. "We can skip the ice cream and go straight home. I'll bet you have homework." I glance up in the rearview mirror at him. I swear the kid is seven going on seventeen. I don't know how Nikita and Lucy handle him. Next time, Nikita should ask Madisyn, Hannah, or someone else with a kid to do the after-school pickup. While their kids are too young for elementary school, at least they know how to deal with kids.

Zion's eyes widen, giving a long side glance out the window. That seems to shut his ass up.

I'm about at my wit's end.

I should have gotten more sleep last night with Savannah. Not that I regret going home with her and spending the night. Watching her sleep had been the morning's highlight since I woke up.

"Ice cream?" Zion quips. This time the kid is quite a bit calmer. Like he's realized he's tried my patience, and I'm about to blow up at him. He probably gets that a lot.

"Yeah, I'll get you a single scoop." I'm not sure the kid deserves it, but I did make him a promise when I convinced him to get into the back seat. I'm not a man to break my word, no matter how small or insignificant it may seem.

———

There's no parking directly outside the ice cream shop. We park several blocks away. The kid grabs my hand right before we cross the street at the traffic light. The city is bustling with the rush hour crowd, and while I'm not used to holding such a tiny hand, I'm as good as dead if I lose the kid.

As we head the last block toward the ice cream shop, I swear I catch sight of her long blonde hair.

Savannah? I blink rapidly. I doubt it's her. Unless she's following me, she doesn't seem to notice me as she hurries into a nearby coffee shop.

"I need to make a stop first," I say.

"But ice cream," the seven-year-old whines.

"We will, kid. Just give me a minute." I practically drag Zion to hurry with me across the street as we head inside the coffee shop. I'm not inconspicuous, but I'm not trying to be. I can order myself a coffee.

Zion grumbles but relents as I usher him inside the small café. The working crowd mainly occupies a few tables and chairs as they type away at their laptops and sip their overpriced coffee.

He drops my hand, no longer finding it necessary to cling to me, and I'm eternally grateful. I'm not used to being around kids. Being an only child, it's not like I had a younger sibling I was forced to babysit.

"I want ice cream," Zion whines.

"That'll be our next stop," I say. There's no sign of Savannah, which is odd considering she waltzed into the café. Well, some blonde woman with her height and build did. I swore it was her.

But there's no sign of her or anyone else fitting her description. Maybe the blonde worked here and slipped into the back to get ready? I stalk up to the counter and order a small coffee, black. I don't want anything fancy.

Zion is at my side, studying the muffins and scones on display. "Can I have one?" he asks, pointing at the sweet treat.

"That depends. Would you rather have that or ice cream?"

"Ice cream," he says in his sweet, innocent, high-pitched voice. There's a grin on his face like he knows he's not supposed to have either so close to dinner, but he's getting away with breaking the rules.

Yeah, I'm the rule breaker.

If I mess up the kid, Nikita won't ask me to handle babysitting duty. Not bad. I don't want to see him get hurt. But maybe too much sugar will bounce him off the walls when we get back to the compound.

Assuming Nikita and Lucy will be back home by the time we arrive.

He'd better be. I didn't sign up for babysitting duty. I need to get back to the club to handle the accounts before the guests start pouring in and the dancers have to get ready.

I pull out a twenty and pay the cashier when I hear Savannah's voice from behind.

"Are you following me?" she asks.

"I could ask the same about you," I say, glancing at her over my shoulder.

She presses her lips tight, and her eyes narrow, forcing a smile. What the hell is she hiding?

"I was using the bathroom," she says and points toward the darkened hallway where the single-occupancy bathroom is situated. Savannah glances down at the kid beside me. "You didn't tell me you were a dad."

"He's not my dad," Zion quips before I can answer. "I don't have a dad. My dad came from the bank."

Savannah's brow pinches, confused by his comment, and it's probably for the best. "Where'd you hear that?" I laugh awkwardly at Zion.

"Mommy was talking, and I overheard her. But I don't understand," Zion says.

"Good," I mutter under my breath. "Ask your mom, kid." I don't have it in me to go anywhere further with this conversation.

"So, not your son," Savannah says and offers a smile. She's trying to piece together Zion's relation to me. Well, I'll let her think on it a little while longer. What fun is it to give away all my secrets?

I shuffle out of the way, and Savannah orders the fanciest coffee imaginable while I wait for the barista to finish preparing my drink. It's taking longer than it should have since I ordered it black. Do they have to go and grow the damn coffee beans?

"Order for Anton," the barista says, handing me the black coffee. The paper exterior is already hot, indicating the coffee will be steaming when I take a sip.

"Can we go for ice cream now?" Zion whines. The kid is losing his patience, and I don't blame him.

"Yeah," I say. I glance back at Savannah and offer a weak smile. "I'll see you tonight."

"Bye," she says and gives a wave to the little boy.

I head with Zion for the door, and a gentleman in a business suit exits and holds the door for us. I can't help but stare. Where the hell was he seated? I glanced over at everyone in the café but hadn't noticed him.

Weird.

————

I'm relieved when I get to drop Zion off at the compound and Hannah offers to keep an eye on him. He runs to the playroom, his fingers still sticky from his devoured raspberry ice cream. The kid also made a mess over his school uniform and my backseat.

But I don't dare want to admit it was nice parading him around downtown. I had a few single ladies smile at me, and Savannah's expression when she thought I was the kid's father was the icing on the cake.

I head straight for the office, which happens to be at the club, loosening my tie and taking off my jacket when I arrive. The air is stuffy. I double-check the thermostat and shake my head in dismay. Who the hell turned it off?

Guests don't want to be sweating their asses off while getting lap dances. I adjust the thermostat and grab a bottle of water from the mini-fridge in Nikita's office. He won't miss it. I doubt he'll even be in today, given he spent the afternoon with Lucy at the hospital.

"Is the thermostat broken?" Dmitri asks. His face is red, and sweat is coating his brow. He's underboss to Mikhail and helps with the club on an as-needed basis, which lately means working every night at Club Sage.

"Some asshole turned the unit off last night," I say as I head toward the back, where it requires a key to enter the basement. All our money laundering and record-keeping are done below the club, out of sight. The door is locked, and no one is permitted downstairs during club business hours. The last thing we want is anyone suspecting what we're up to or sneaking down and catching a peek.

Dmitri throws his arms up in the air. "Wasn't me, but the club was comfortable last night. Are you sure it's not broken?"

"We just put a new HVAC system in during the renovations. It had better not be fucking broken," I grumble and reach for my cold water, taking a swig.

I head for the basement, and Dmitri follows behind. I unlock the door, and he shuts it behind us. The door locks automatically, and we head down the stairwell. Already, a dozen associates are handling the funds from yesterday, mixing the club money with our funds from other illegal activities.

Dmitri and I ensure that the operation runs smoothly and that our associates aren't stealing from us.

The air downstairs is much more comfortable below ground. It's not as stifling, but it's warmer than usual. "Who the hell turned off the air conditioning?"

Silence fills the space. No one admits to what they've done, and why should they? You don't fuck around when it comes to the bratva, no matter how small or insignificant you think the error might be.

I examine the room. A few men refuse to meet my gaze, cowering out of fear. No one confesses, and I'm not about to put a bullet in someone's head over the club's temperature this time, but if it was intentional and they're attempting to sabotage the reopening, then they're dead.

I can't think of any of Mikhail's men who would want to sabotage the club, but the mafia and cartel would gladly watch us suffer.

Dmitri's jaw is tight. He says nothing and stalks past the men as they resume their activities counting the money. The man is all muscle, so he's been working the door as an extra bodyguard to keep the club safe after our intrusion a few months ago.

I grab the ledger off the desk and return it to my office. I shut the door behind myself and slam into Savannah as I round the corner.

"What are you doing here?" The words come out before an apology for practically knocking her over. However, I wasn't expecting anyone else to be here yet.

"I was looking for you," Savannah says.

I grip the ledger tight and wander to my office. I can't let Savannah become a distraction. "You aren't due here for another hour," I say and glance at my watch.

It's less than an hour until the girls start showing up. My day was shot when I had to pick up Zion from school and then make a few quick stops in the city.

"I was hoping I could talk to you," Savannah says. She stands at the entrance to my office like she's waiting for an invitation.

The girl has me tied around her finger. I should tell her to get ready and leave me alone, but I don't.

"I have work to do," I say.

She presses her lips together and gives a weak nod. "Cute nephew you have," she says, taking a stab at the relationship between Zion and myself.

He does refer to me as his Uncle Anton, so I'll give her that one. "Thanks." He may not be a blood relative, but he's the family of the bratva, and that's good enough for me.

I sit behind my desk, the ledger closed, but hiding it is pointless. I place it on my desk, my hand covering it, although it's shut and the dark brown cover reveals nothing out of the ordinary.

"I'm sorry, it's clear you're busy, and I'm interrupting," Savannah says, finally getting the hint that I don't have time to stand around and chit chat.

I work long days and late nights for the bratva. The job is practically around the clock. I don't get to walk away after a shift and turn off that part of my life. "Come in; close the door," I say. Something about her makes me not want to push her away. Maybe it's because I haven't had a relationship in ages.

Usually, a girl shies away when she hears I help with Club Sage and am around strippers every day. Most of the girls I date don't have enough confidence to handle that I can see a girl in a thong and not want to fuck her.

Well, that is until I met Savannah.

The girl is like fire, and I want to play with her even though I know it's deadly and dangerous and I'll get burned.

A little pain never hurt anyone.

"Are you sure?" Savannah asks, but she steps into my office and closes the door. She sits in the chair opposite my desk, straight across from me. It's reminiscent of our first encounter yesterday when she interviewed with me. Except this time, she's not climbing on my desk and giving me a show.

Too bad. That was quite an enjoyable afternoon. However, I look forward to catching a glimpse of her dancing tonight.

"You're here early. Any reason?" I ask. I grab a pen from the desk and open the ledger. From her position, she can't see the information. Besides, there's nothing of any interest to her.

I need to get a little work done now if I plan on watching her dance tonight. I glance up, waiting for her to answer, pen in hand. She can't tell me she's bored and decided to show up to work early. That's an excuse. I need to hear the real reason she's here; I'm sure it has little to do with me. We only slept together once. We're barely anything.

"Honestly, I was curious about the kid, but since you're his uncle, you answered my question."

"You came into work early to ask me about Zion?" I put the pen down. I don't believe it. "You're a terrible liar," I say.

Savannah's cheeks burn, and she glances down at her lap. She twirls a strand of hair around her finger and glances back at me with a shy smile.

I don't fall for her shy routine.

"Out with it," I say.

"I wanted to ask you on a date," Savannah says.

I clear my throat. That was not what I was expecting. I'm not sure what I thought she wanted when she came into my office, but a date? "We have to keep what we have between us quiet," I say.

"I know. I just meant that maybe we could grab a bite to eat after work?"

She wants a repeat of last night. Okay, I can go for that, given that it means I wind up in her bed. "I'd like that," I say. I suppose this isn't a one-night stand. I wasn't sure last night, after we slept together, if she wanted me to leave and just keep things professional between us.

But already, I like being around her, and while I shouldn't have my head in the clouds, it's dangerous. The girl has no idea what I do for a living outside of working at the club.

I glance at the ledger on my desk. I need to review the numbers and follow up on that background check we ran on Savannah as a new hire. It'd be good to reassure myself that she's not mixed up with the Italian Mafia or Colombian Cartel. Both are dangerous organizations, and while we've established a truce with the Italians, the cartel we took down several months ago. It's only a matter of time before they retaliate when a new leader rises.

"Anything else?" I ask.

She shakes her head. "I just wanted to make sure I stole a minute with you alone before the other girls came in. I don't want them to talk."

"I appreciate that," I say, relieved that she, too, wants to keep what is happening between us a secret.

Savannah doesn't get up from the chair. "What are you working on?" she asks. Her tone doesn't show like she's that interested, just trying to make polite conversation.

I don't want to be rude or belittle her by pointing out that it's nothing that she'd understand. "Just going over the numbers. Boring stuff," I say.

"I went to college for accounting," she chimes.

"And you dropped out because you partied more than you went to class," I say, recalling what she told me.

She shrugs, knowing that I'm right. "Yeah, I probably am not much help, but I'd love to learn. I'm more of a hands-on learner than grasping what is read in a textbook. I prefer real-world experience."

"I'll keep that in mind," I say.

Savannah stands and points behind her at the door. "I suppose I should go and start getting ready."

"Good idea."

She stands and heads for the door. "Do you want me to leave your door open or closed?"

"Closed," I say.

The moment the door shuts, I return my attention to the books. I manage to get in two hours of examining the books and working on a separate ledger for our taxes when there's a firm knock at the door, and Nikita strolls in uninvited.

"I didn't expect to see you in the office today." I glance up briefly before returning my attention to my work. "How's the wife?"

"Lucy is fine. She just sprained her ankle. The doctor wrapped it, but she'll be good as new soon enough."

"That's good to hear," I say, my pen poised over the page as I stop and listen to Nikita.

"Thanks again for taking Zion home this afternoon. I realized I forgot to leave you the booster seat. I have a spare in the office closet upstairs if you ever need to pick him up again."

I hope he's not making this a habit or a new part of my job responsibility. "Yeah, sure. As long as you don't mind that I give the kid ice cream on the way home."

"You didn't," Nikita deadpans. He doesn't believe me.

"The kid didn't tell you?" I'm surprised Zion was able to keep a secret. I suppose Hannah had him change out of his school uniform when he got home.

"Zion usually can't keep a secret," Nikita says. "But he forgot to mention the ice cream. Anything else I should know?"

"I swung by the bar and took him for his first beer."

"Now I know you're joking." Nikita folds his arms across his chest defensively, but he doesn't seem angry with me. "Thanks for looking out for him and helping. I know you're not fond of kids."

"I never said that." I put my pen down. "I've never been around kids."

"Are you offering to babysit?" Nikita quips. "Zion had wonderful things to say about you. Gave you five stars."

"Oh, you're rating me now?" It would be like Nikita to try turning this around and convince me to watch the kid while he goes out with Lucy. I don't comment on his question, not wanting to tell my boss no way in hell.

"Zion's words, not mine. I'll let you get back to it but consider my request. We're willing to pay."

I shake my head. "No, thanks. I'd rather be attacked by scorpions and tarantulas."

Nikita grimaces. "Ouch. Well, wear a condom, so you don't have a little scorpion running around."

I snort under my breath. He couldn't know about Savannah. It's only been a day since she was hired. "I'll keep that in mind next time I go out."

"Right, you do that," Nikita says with a smirk.

There's no way he knows what happened with Savannah last night, or relatively, very early this morning. He was long gone before we left together. Unless Dmitri said something; he was the last to leave. He could have seen me give Savannah a ride.

I'll have to be more careful around her while at the club. The last thing in the world I want is for the other girls to give her a hard time or for them to think that I'm giving her special treatment.

Nikita shuts the door on his way out of my office. I glance at my watch. I need to be on the floor, keeping an eye on the patrons and the girls, making sure the place is running smoothly. I open the desk drawer and shove the ledger inside, locking the drawer before I head out of my office.

I shut the office door and step out of the hallway to the lounge. The tables are full, and the waitresses are bustling around. Lucy isn't working tonight, which is not surprising considering her recent injury. The place is busy and it's only the middle of the week.

I'm grateful the air conditioning is pumping through the club, and the climate is comfortable for everyone. Bailey is center stage, while Savannah is nowhere in sight. She's probably giving a private dance to a guest.

There are cameras in every private booth for the girls' protection. I slink off to the control room to see what's happening with Savannah. We have security who watches the monitors to ensure the girls' safety and that they're not compromised. They're not allowed to go home with any clientele or have sex with anyone while at the club.

We're a high-end gentleman's club, not a whorehouse.

I slip into the control room and shut the door behind myself. There are a dozen cameras that watch the lounge, and there are sofas, tables, and platforms where the girls dance. I focus on the private booths, not the VIP rooms. It's more than likely that she's in a booth with a client.

My mouth is parched when I glance at the screen. The man she's grinding against, I recognize him.

I inhale a sharp breath. It's the same gentleman from the café this afternoon. I hadn't noticed the one in the overpriced suit at a table. That can't be a coincidence.

FIVE

SAVANNAH

"You shouldn't be here," I whisper against his ear.

Special Agent James Lexington is my handler. I'm supposed to report anything that happens at the club, and I haven't given him much information. I met up with him earlier at the café, when I nearly got caught by Anton.

How the hell had he found our meeting place?

We'll have to change it, someplace even more public where we're less likely to run into Anton. Not that I expected he'd show up with a kid to the café! I swear he followed me, but when did he manage to pick up his nephew if that were the case?

When I read his background, he didn't have any siblings, which makes having a nephew odd. Maybe it's one of the kids from another member of the bratva? It's not a question I can ask without Anton discovering that I know who he is, and it might reveal my true identity.

I straddle James in the small booth. The room is overzealous with red: red curtains, a red sofa, and even red overhead lighting to set the mood. There's a coffee table in front of the couch, allowing me a platform in the small space if I choose to dance for him.

There are cameras in every nook and cranny of this place, but I'm not sure about audio, so I have to tread carefully.

He's my first private dance. Anyone else, and I'd suspect they could be part of the bratva, testing me. But James is here on pleasure, not business. If it were strictly business, he'd have found a way to talk to me in the lounge or slipped me a note, not paid for a dance.

I start on the coffee table. It's made of wood and easily holds my weight as my platforms click over the material underneath.

"What would you like me to do for you?" I ask, keeping my voice loud enough for the microphones, if there are any, or the outside bodyguards, to hear the interaction. We're not in a private suite. The walls on either side of the couch are shimmery red curtains.

I'm paid by the minute at five-minute intervals, so dragging out everything is encouraged. One of the girls gave me a quick tutorial on making the men beg for what they want and, if they don't ask, dragging it out longer to make more money.

"I want to see you naked," James whispers, staring at me. He loosens his tie, and his jaw is practically on the floor.

"I'll bet you do," I tease with a smirk. There's no way in hell he's got enough cash to earn him a peek at my pink bits. But my job is to tease him, excite him, and make it look believable for the cameras.

"What's your favorite part of my body?" I ask and let my fingers trail over my chest, attempting to entice him.

He croaks and clears his throat. James is trying to stay professional, but he's long since lost that round.

He shoves a handful of ones at me, and I shake my head. "It'll cost you more than that if you want a peek at anything."

My fingers rake through James' hair as he leans into me, and his eyes are closed. He's smitten. He doesn't have a wife at home. No kids. He's single, and I've always thought the man preferred work over a woman, but honestly, I'm not so convinced.

I've never seen this side of him, and part of me feels bad for the man. Another part is eager to take his cash. If he's stupid enough to wander into the club and request a dance from me, he will pay the price heavily.

I lower my voice. If there is an audio recording, the music overhead will drown out my whisper. "What are you doing here?"

The FBI shouldn't be here, investigating or sneaking around while I'm undercover. They could blow the entire operation. "New meeting point," James answers just as quietly.

Couldn't he have found another way to tell me of the location change?

His hand comes out, and I push it back down onto the sofa. "No touching," I warn, my voice loud enough for him and the bodyguard to hear.

"Sorry," James is quick to apologize.

I grind my hips against his crotch, and he's not sporting his weapon. I try to ignore the bump I feel and the fact that this man is my colleague and one of my closest allies at the bureau. This has to look believable in case anyone is watching.

But at the same time, my stomach is in knots. What if Anton is watching? Will he recognize him from this morning? Will he remember that James held the door for him at the café?

Anton isn't an idiot. He won't strike it up as a coincidence. This little mishap could ruin the investigation or get me killed.

"You shouldn't be here," I whisper into his ear. "He'll recognize you." I climb down from the table and straddle him.

"I doubt it. There are over eight million people in New York City. I'm just another face."

James is cocky, and it could end up with me getting interrogated or tortured by the bratva. "Where are we meeting?" I ask, wanting this dance to be over. The longer he stays in the booth, the greater the chance Anton will discover him at the club. He needs to leave.

"Here," James says with a sly grin.

"Not going to work. He's already seen your face. You're lucky you're not dead. Send Barrett."

"You want to dance for our boss?" James asks, and I swear if he speaks any louder, I'll have no choice but to murder him.

"Anton's keeping a close eye on me," I whisper as my fingernails tease through his scalp. "Barrett can slip me a note. But you need to give me one of your business cards. Put it between the folded bills," I say.

His eyes tighten, but he doesn't answer. I climb off his lap and hold out my hand, demanding payment. We're paid in five-minute increments, and while most clients I would keep teasing, getting them to pay me even more, James needs to leave.

I climb off his lap, and he shucks a couple of extra twenties at me, grumbling.

"You aren't to come back here," I say as James stands and pushes aside the thick red curtain, exiting the room.

I wait for James to head down the hallway before I push the plush curtain aside and come face-to-face with Anton.

I press my lips together and give a bashful smile. "Are you here for a dance?" I pray that he didn't hear a word between James and me.

Anton pushes forward into the booth, not the least bit apologetic in his demeanor, and I stumble back toward the couch, keeping him from knocking into me. The space isn't huge, and he's taking up as much of it as possible.

"I saw that man earlier; who is he to you?" Anton pushes me down onto the sofa and traps me from leaving the room.

I laugh, shrugging off his question and ignoring his bruteness. "Are you going to dance for me?" I tug my bottom lip between my teeth. I'd love to see Anton dance, but I don't imagine he would, and certainly not while on camera.

His nostrils flare as he sneers at my suggestion, and his hand wraps around my neck, enough to cut off blood supply, but he's not crushing my windpipe. He's done this before. "Tell me, *kitten*, who was that man?"

My arms flail as I whack him on the side of the head, attempting to break free. He releases his hold, pinning me with his stare.

"FBI," I gasp. My heart pounds wildly against my chest as I catch my breath.

"He's with the FBI?" Anton glances me up and down, satisfied that I'm not lying. "What did he want?"

I'm not afraid of Anton. I should be considering he could kill and dispose of me, and no one would ever find my body.

I reveal the business card to Anton, proving that James is a federal agent. "He told me that you're Russian Mafia," I say.

"We prefer the term bratva." Anton's gaze tightens as he holds my stare. "What else did he tell you, *kitten*?"

"That I shouldn't trust you."

Anton chuckles under his breath. "You shouldn't. I'm a dangerous man."

"You don't scare me," I whisper, climbing onto his lap and straddling him.

"There are cameras," Anton warns.

But I don't care.

Let them watch.

"You've never been into voyeurism?" I tease and drag my fingers through his hair and down his jawline, gentle and slow. I don't want him to feel I'm a threat to him or the men he works with.

He grumbles and pushes me off his body. "You're distracting me." He stands and steps on the other side of the coffee table, keeping a solid distance between us. Anton rubs his forehead before stroking his jaw. He's restless and bothered by the information that I've given him.

Is he afraid that I'll tempt him if we're too close?

I need him to trust me, and if he thinks the FBI is watching him and I'm an ally, maybe he'll give me a little more responsibility and divulge some of the secrets he keeps.

"If you don't have anything else, I have more clients to entertain," I say. I stand, and he snarls at me.

"Sit back down."

I slump back down onto the sofa. I can't read if he's jealous or angry. He stalks toward the couch and shoves the table out of the way, coming to stand in front of me.

"Prove your loyalty," he commands.

I stare up at him. "Do you want a blow job?"

He growls and grabs me by the hair, pulling me down to lie on the couch as he straddles me. "Don't ever offer a man that in my club!"

With him holding a fistful of my hair, I can't get away or fight him. And I'm cautious about how I fight, knowing I could easily give away who I am or my FBI training.

"I want your obedience and your submission," he demands. His left hand grips my hair while his right closes in around my neck.

"You have it," I whisper, staring up at him.

He doesn't squeeze. He finds my pulse point, his eyes entirely on mine. "You don't fear me," he says, the realization dawning on him that I'm not fighting to get away to break free or beg for my life.

"I have no reason to fear you. Should I?" I ask. My life is in his hands. It's a dangerous game, but he'll never open up to me if I don't show him that I trust him.

His mouth presses against mine, and his tongue pushes past my lips. If it were any other man at the club, I'd be repulsed by such behavior, but with Anton, I want him to touch me.

He's fully dressed, but I can feel his cock pressed against me. "I want you to fuck me," I whisper, trying to keep my voice down so that only he can hear me.

Anton growls before releasing his hold and climbing off me. Sweat beads on his forehead. The room is stifling. "Get back to work," he orders and pushes the curtains aside as he disappears out of the room.

———

The rest of the evening is far less eventful. I give a few lap dances, but none are overly memorable for me after what transpired earlier. I'm still ablaze from

Anton discovering James and questioning me about him.

As the night winds down and the club closes, I head to the dressing room to change into my jeans and pink shirt. I grab my small duffel containing an extra pair of clothes, my makeup, and all my face wash products. I have glitter caked onto my skin, unlike last night when I toned down the makeup since I hadn't brought much of my own.

My clutch is tucked deep into my duffel, along with my phone. I'll grab my cell phone and order a rideshare service if Anton has already left. But I'm hoping that he will wait for me.

Exiting the dressing room, I head down the elongated hallway for his office and give a prompt knock. The door squeaks open. It wasn't shut very tight.

Anton is situated behind his desk. His sleeves are rolled up, and his jacket is slung on the chair opposite him. I don't want to be presumptuous. We may have talked about grabbing a bite to eat after the club closed, but things change.

James showed up.

I didn't intend to tell him that James is FBI, but I suspected I might need to do something if Anton has any suspicions. That's why I insisted James leave me his business card, as a reassurance that I was telling the truth.

Anton's brow is tight, and he looks a bit confused.

"It's time already?" He glances at the watch on his wrist and puts his pen down. He shuts the ledger he's working on and opens the top desk drawer, shoving it inside. He locks the drawer behind him and stands.

Anton comes around from behind his desk, rolling down his sleeves. He grabs his suit coat and slips it back on as he escorts me outside.

The other girls have already left. The place is bare, and as we exit outside, I notice that there's only one vehicle in the lot, Anton's.

He unlocks the doors to the SUV, and I open the backseat, putting my duffel on the floor behind my seat. I carefully maneuver the tracking device. I had kept it nestled in my palm under the duffel strap.

I shove it under the passenger seat. Hopefully, no one will ever notice it.

I slam the back door and jump into the front seat, securing my seatbelt.

"Ready?" he asks. The engine runs, and he strums his hands on the steering wheel, waiting attentively for me.

"Same place as last night?" I'm not sure what's open at this hour. Most of the city is asleep, and the few open places aren't in the best parts of town.

"I have someplace else in mind. Do you trust me?"

I inhale sharply. "I do."

"Good." He heads out of the parking lot, not giving me any indication of where we're going. The city disappears as we head farther out of town.

Is he planning on taking me someplace remote and killing me? Has he figured out that I'm an FBI agent?

As I shift in the front seat, I try not to show discomfort—my stomach grumbles.

"We're almost there," he says.

I don't point out that there hasn't been anything for miles. It's open roads, forests, and trees surrounding us—the perfect place for a body dump.

There's a weapon buried at the bottom of my duffel bag, but that's in the backseat. "What are we doing out here, Anton?" The smile has left my face, and it has been replaced with dread.

"You look worried," he says and glances at me briefly before returning his attention to the road. "Why? Don't you trust me?"

"There are no restaurants open out here." I don't bother mentioning that it's late, and the sun will soon be coming up.

"There's a protein bar in the glovebox."

I open the glove box, and sure enough, there's a protein bar stashed inside. That's not the only thing I notice peeking out from under his registration and paperwork. I also see the glistening metal of a handgun.

I don't comment on the gun, pretending not to notice it when I grab the protein bar and shut the glovebox. I can't snatch the gun without Anton noticing, and the last thing I want is for him to drive us off the road, wrestling me for the weapon.

"Do you want half?" I offer him part of the snack.

"No, thanks."

He pulls off the road onto a small pathway. It's narrow and dark. There haven't been any vehicles for miles, but it's also the middle of the night. When he gets to the intended destination, he kills the engine.

"We're here," he says.

I glance at him and back at the glovebox. I have only one chance. Yanking the compartment open, I grab the gun, click off the safety, and point it at him. I'm not going down without a fight.

SIX

ANTON

"What the hell are you doing, Savannah?" It's the first time I haven't called her by the little pet name that I've bestowed on her.

Why the fuck did she steal my gun? And why is she pointing it at me?

"You tell me! You brought me to the middle of nowhere."

I really wish that I hadn't loaded the gun with bullets. She's cocked the safety off, so she seems to know what she's doing, and her hands aren't shaking. Is it the adrenaline or something else?

"I brought you so we could go camping," I say. "The gear is in the trunk. You can have a look if you'd like."

She glances from me to the back of the SUV. She can't see the trunk's contents from here, and I didn't bring that much stuff. I was planning on roughing it with her. I had wanted to sleep under the stars and get to know her but figured a tent would come in handy if the bugs got to be too much.

"Really? Camping on a second date?"

"I didn't know we were dating," I say and quirk a grin, attempting to disarm her emotionally.

Hopefully, I can retrieve the gun if I make her realize I'm not that bad of a guy. She's probably flustered after that stupid FBI agent showing up at the club, putting scary thoughts into her head about who we are and what we do.

"I just thought," her nose scrunches and the look of irritation crosses her face, "you brought me out here to kill me!"

"Why would I do that?" I ask, my voice calm and even. That FBI agent got inside her head. "Is that what that man told you? That I murder people."

"Not in so many words," Savannah whispers. Her brow furrows, and she slowly lowers the gun. I grab it from her and put the safety back on before shoving it back into the glovebox.

"He was following me this morning," I say, trying to explain what I know to her as best as I can. "I saw him at the café when we bumped into each other. No way it was a coincidence." It's the first time I recall seeing him before Club Sage. "He must have seen us together and figured he'd get to me through you."

I need to be more careful, especially if the feds are snooping around, following my ass and harassing the girls at the club.

"I didn't tell him anything," Savannah says, her voice softer, calmer. "I'm sorry I pulled your gun on you."

"So am I." I run a hand through my unkempt hair and give a throaty laugh. I never thought I'd see the day when one of the dancers snatched my gun and had the opportunity to kill me. I also never expected to sleep with one of them.

I exhale a heavy breath. "Come look at the stars with me," I say and climb out of the vehicle. The air in the

SUV is heavy and oppressive from what just transpired. I need a little distance and space, not necessarily from Savannah but from all of it.

I want to leave it behind.

But I can't.

I'm part of the bratva. They're my brothers, and I will never be able to escape their clutches. Not that it's all bad. I like working for Nikita. And Mikhail is a fine Pakhan. I have no complaints about him running the show. It would just be nice not to look over my shoulder and worry that my ass could get thrown in prison for the shit I've done.

Another life, maybe. If you believe in that sort of thing.

I open the trunk, and the lid lifts, revealing the contents stored inside. Savannah comes around the passenger side to stand with me, taking notice of the tent. "How'd you know I love camping?"

"I took a guess," I say. She could have been the kind of woman who hates the outdoors, but even if that were the case, we could lie out under the stars and stare up at the night sky. I've never had a woman say no to doing that with me. Not that it's a regular occurrence, but I was young once—what feels like a lifetime ago.

I grab the bag with the tent and poles inside and bring it out of the SUV. There's a clearing in the forest, a perfect spot to camp under the stars. The tent I got allows one to sky watch while being inside, perfect so that we can fall asleep under the stars.

Using the vehicle's headlights, within a matter of minutes, I have the tent set up, and I toss in a sleeping bag and open it up for us to lie on together. I grab a second sleeping bag and open it up as a blanket if it gets any chillier.

"Come lie under the stars with me." I don't wait for Savannah to answer. I grab her hand and tug her to follow me into the tent.

We shuffle onto the sleeping bag, and I lay my head on the plush, oversized pillow. Savannah curls right up beside me, sharing my pillow as we stare at the night sky.

I want her to relax and unwind. But I also want her to tell me everything the FBI agent said to her tonight. I need to know how much the feds know and what they have on us, if anything. I'm guessing not much, or they'd raid the place.

She stares up at the sky. There's a heaviness that looms over her.

Is it because she's tired?

It's well beyond the early morning hours, and soon the night sky will offer a beautiful sunrise that will be difficult to see among the trees. The clearing gives us the perfect view straight above but obstructs everything around us, with dancing shadows and branches twisting for miles in every direction.

I run my fingers over her arm, a gentle caress over her bare skin as I pull her closer and roll onto my side. I want to kiss her, devour her, and show her what it's like to be worshipped by a man obsessed with her.

"I'm sorry that I doubted you," Savannah says, her voice barely above a whisper.

"He got into your head, that's all." It's not as though Savannah has been working with me for years or is part of the bratva. She's probably the easiest to turn, and that's what that stupid federal agent had been counting on.

Savannah emits a heavy sigh. "Are you dangerous?"

Her question catches me off guard. I had expected her to ask about the business, if I've murdered anyone before or even what we do as bratva.

"I'd never hurt you, *kitten*," I say. "You shouldn't fear me." I don't point out that if she betrayed me and spilled my secrets to the FBI, I'd have no choice but to hurt her.

I am dangerous.

Ruthless.

Cruel.

Savage.

I've been called all sorts of names in all the years I've been loyal to Mikhail and the bratva. But I don't murder for sport. I'm not an animal. My decisions are thought out and planned.

"But you are dangerous," she says and turns her head, eyes on me.

"I won't lie to you." There's no reason to hide the truth from her about who I am. That stupid federal agent already spilled my secrets. "I've done things

I'm not proud of, but I always protect my family first and foremost."

What else did he tell her?

My stomach flops as I stare at her and realize she has far too many clothes on, and if she's been accosted by the FBI, she could be wearing a wire.

There were no vehicles following us on our way. There's no one out here for miles in any direction. But if she's recording our conversation, she could hand it over to the feds.

I have to know that I can trust her.

My fingers skim over her hips and up her stomach, trailing a rough, warm path against her skin. I need to see that she's not wired and has nothing to hide from me.

I gently allow my palm to graze her stomach before guiding my hand under her shirt. There is plenty of space for her to have a wire taped or tucked into her bra.

I feel nothing but soft skin and hear a moan slip from the back of her throat. "You would never betray me, *kitten*, would you?"

My palm rubs over her breast. She's wearing a bra, unlike last night when she'd been dressed down. Not that she's sporting a gown, but she's in jeans, instead of sweats, and a nice shirt.

I don't get my hopes up thinking she's dressed this way for me. That would be ludicrous. I barely know the girl, but I'm memorizing every inch of her body as I massage one of her breasts and unclasp her bra with the other hand.

The material feels thin and lacy. It's too dark to see what it looks like under the night sky. The moon is a crescent, barely offering any light cast through the trees.

Did she wear that for me?

I rid her of her shirt, lifting it over her head, and the bra glides off her arms, revealing no wire. I'm relieved that she's not secretly working with the feds.

Savannah loosens my tie and slowly frees the buttons of my dress shirt. I slip my suit jacket off and lay it beside us on the tent's floor. I should have changed into something more practical for camping, but I didn't want to clue Savannah in to where we were going.

Besides, it's not as though we're hiking or spending hours on the trails. We'll pack up the tent, head out to breakfast, and return to the city tomorrow.

Savannah climbs onto my hips, straddling me as she hurriedly works the buttons free and peels my shirt off before bending down and covering my lips with hers.

She tastes sweet, like honey and almonds. I nip at her lips and roll around, wrestling her beneath me.

Her eyes shine in the darkness as I lift my hips and unbutton her jeans, guiding them down and off. Her panties are made of the same material as her bra. There's lace along the sides and silk at the front.

My fingers itch to rip her panties off, but instead, I drag out the moment, wanting to hear her moans and pleas. I like watching her restless and needy at my hands. Something is satisfying in knowing that I've made her that way.

"Anton," she purrs my name in that sultry, sexy voice that sends a jolt of electricity riveting inside of me.

I want to set her ablaze, screaming my name, all inhibitions gone. Her focus is on me, undressing me, helping me out of my pants so that I'm naked along with her. I shuck my pants to the side and settle between her thighs.

Her fingernails scratch at my back as she grows restless with anticipation. No doubt she's tired, and there are still specks of glitter on her cheek, hair, and probably all over her body. There's not a shower at the club, and she didn't have time to run home and get cleaned up. I'll see glitter for the next week on me, and I don't give a fuck.

I just want to be buried deep inside of her.

I crave her touch, her body nestled with mine. After our experience together last night, she's like a drug, and I need my next fix.

Will she give me what I so desperately need, *her*?

My mouth grazes her stomach as I nip and kiss her hips, pulling her panties down with my teeth.

She gasps, and her fingers tangle in my hair while lifting her hips for me to maneuver her panties off. I growl at her eagerness and explore every inch of her body, tasting her and listening to her soft pants and pleas as she begs for more.

The moans and sounds she makes drive me wild, and before long, she's clenching around my fingers. I want to be buried deep inside of her. I climb back up her body, ridding myself of my last shred of clothes, my boxers. I reach for my wallet to grab a condom before positioning myself at her entrance.

Her legs are bent, and her eyes struggle to remain open. Each breath is heavy and raspy as she waits for me.

I don't want to crush her. She's delicate compared to me, sweet and perfect. I fill her, burying deep inside. As I enter her, she moans and the sounds she makes drive me wild.

Each thrust grows more intense.

Hotter.

Vibrant.

Like fuel thrown on a fire.

Her fingernails scratch my back and down to my ass, marking me.

The impending explosion comes crashing down. Her insides quiver, and she tightens and shudders, spasming around me. I'm with her, on the edge of oblivion, falling and gasping for air as my heart slams against my ribcage.

Perfection.

———

As the weeks pass, there's no sign of the FBI guy. He doesn't return to the club, and I've been at Savannah's apartment every night, staking the place to ensure that the feds aren't following her. And as a bonus, I get to be tangled with her in the sheets.

I considered going to Mikhail and requesting a low-level associate to tail her and ensure she isn't being harassed during the day, but that would imply that the feds are an issue. And I don't want to believe that they are. She told Agent James Lexington that she wasn't interested in working for them, and they left her alone.

At least, that's the story she's given me, and I've seen no proof otherwise.

But I'm leery and cautious.

Because if Savannah isn't working for the feds, then they'll just target another girl at the club. I head up the stairs for Nikita's office.

I knock promptly and then open the door when I hear a muffled, "Come in."

"You have a sec?" I ask. Whether he does or not, I'm interrupting him. I've debated whether I should let Nikita know about that weasel harassing one of our girls. But telling him might let it slip that Savannah and I have been hooking up just about every night for the past month, maybe longer.

I haven't been keeping count. I can't remember the exact date we met, only what transpired. I'm not a sentimental guy. I've never celebrated Valentine's Day or sent flowers as a grand romantic gesture.

"Good, I've wanted to have a word with you," Nikita says. "Take a seat." He gestures toward the chair opposite his desk.

I do as he instructs. Nikita clasps his hands together on the wood desk. "You and Savannah seem close."

We always are the last to leave, and Savannah comes in early to work. I've always assumed it was to spend a few minutes with me, but it isn't necessary. She could come in late, and I wouldn't give her a hard time.

But maybe I should.

Perhaps the others are growing suspicious. Is that what Nikita is saying?

"I'm close with all the dancers. I like to think that they can come to me if they have a problem."

Nikita's eyes tighten. He doesn't buy a line of my bullshit.

"Admit it. You're fucking the new hire."

"You're wrong." The lie falls so easily from my lips, I don't even believe it. It shouldn't matter, except that mixing business and pleasure is frowned upon. There are strict rules about the dancers not fraternizing with the staff.

Mikhail doesn't want a sexual harassment lawsuit and to spend countless dollars on litigation. But Savannah isn't after our money, or even my money, for that matter. She's different from any other girl I've slept with before.

And I've experienced my fair share of women.

"Would you prefer the term dating?" Nikita quips.

"You're mistaken." My jaw is tight. I don't want this to get back to Mikhail or anyone else.

He waves his hand dismissively. I'm not sure he's convinced we're just colleagues, but he doesn't continue the ambush. "All that aside, the girls are coming here tonight."

"What?" His remark has caught me off-guard. Not that it should matter, but I like to be kept informed when the boss comes to the club. It's like rolling out the red carpet for him.

"Madisyn, Hannah, and Lucy. They're celebrating Hannah's engagement."

"At a gentleman's club?"

"You know Mikhail keeps a tight leash on Madisyn. He wants to ensure the girls are safe, and since we don't own a male strip club, this was the next best thing. Anyways, make them feel welcome."

"I'm not stripping for them."

Nikita chuckles at my remark. "I wasn't asking. I don't want to see that, and neither do our clients."

"Good," I say and run a hand through my hair.

"Was there something that you wanted to discuss?" Nikita asks.

"Nothing I can't handle," I say.

Should I mention that the feds have been all over this place, trying to get to me through Savannah? He'll be pissed if he finds out another way, but then I'll have to come clean about sleeping with her.

Is that all we're doing, sleeping together?

It feels like more, but we've been cautious and kept it a secret at my request. And surprisingly, Savannah hasn't pushed for more. I'd have thought she'd have wanted to meet my friends, even suggest staying over at my place, but that conversation hasn't even come up.

And I'm eternally grateful. It's not like I can invite her into the compound. There are rules about that sort of thing. Not that anyone follows them. Nikita and Luka both seemed to break them, and as far as I know, there weren't any dire consequences with Mikhail. But they're closer to him than I am.

I still swing by the compound for fresh clothes, a shower, and sometimes a nap because the woman keeps me up all night. But it's worth it.

She's worth it.

Perhaps that's why Nikita seems to realize I must be hooking up with someone. I rarely come home to sleep at a reasonable hour.

He isn't wrong, but I'm not about to confess that or anything else to him.

"I'll be sure to give the girls a warm welcome," I say and head out of his office, exhaling a sharp breath.

Why am I nervous? It shouldn't matter if he finds out I'm dating one of the girls. He's not going to shoot me over it. Would he fire Savannah or, worse, make me fire her?

Bailey and Ava are dancing on stage. Chloe, Violet, and Missy wander through the club. Chloe and Violet are talking to a small group of men, flirting, teasing, and inviting them for a private dance. Missy is table dancing for one of our regulars. She's trying to entice him to the VIP lounge, not just a private dance.

Savannah is nowhere in sight. I suspect she's giving a lap dance to one of our clients in a private booth. A part of me wants to look, watch the tapes, or wander by the red curtains and listen to the sounds being made.

But I should let her do her job, or Nikita is right; mixing business and pleasure is bad. He'd told me that early on when I was brought in to help with Club Sage. I've always considered him a mentor and friend, not just my tough-ass boss.

There's no sign of Madisyn, Hannah, or Lucy yet. I glance at my watch. Nikita didn't mention what time they'd be arriving, but I'm sure it'll be any minute.

I head for my office and grab my key to unlock the door when I find the handle turns easily.

It's unlocked.

I yank open the door, and Savannah is situated behind my desk, standing over it, the drawer slightly open and the ledger spread out as she examines it.

"What the fuck are you doing?"

SEVEN

SAVANNAH

"Nothing, I mean—"

Oh shit, I am fucked.

I don't have a reasonable excuse for why I was snooping through his office, examining the ledger for evidence.

He slams the door behind himself, and I swear the room shakes. The few pictures on the walls rattle, and it's not from the music pulsating through the club.

"It's not what you think," I say and exhale a calm breath. I need him to believe I'm not betraying him because he'll kill me if he learns the truth.

"Tell me what it is I think," Anton says, and he steps closer, within my grasp. He towers above me and glances briefly to confirm his suspicions that I was examining the ledger.

And it's not just any ledger. It's the one that ties him to money laundering hundreds of thousands through the club. A club of this magnitude, even in New York City, isn't bringing in a solid six figures a week.

Or maybe they are, but they're doing it legally.

Club Sage is dirty, and I can take Anton down.

But my stomach knots at the thought of him discovering who I am and my betrayal. It won't be easy, but I never expected it.

"Remember when I told you I went to college for accounting?"

"Where you dropped out in your first year."

Damn, he remembers. Whoever said that men don't listen? Why couldn't Anton have been one of those men?

"I have a thing for numbers. I like looking at them, examining them, and trying to make sense of them. It's like one of my kinks," I say and wrinkle my nose like I'm telling him a secret.

Anton's face doesn't flinch. There's no smile. "You have a kink for numbers?"

I'm not sure that he believes me.

Hell, I barely believe it myself.

"Spreadsheets, ledgers, they all get me riled up," I say, trying to alleviate his suspicions. "And there's a lot of wealthy men out there tonight. I was trying to get in the mood, and when you weren't in your office—"

"Which you broke into, I might add."

"That's not true." I hold up the key. "You gave me a spare key a couple of nights ago so that I could grab your overnight bag while you handled something downstairs."

He nods briskly, seeming to believe my lie.

"I'm glad I found you. Nikita informed me that we have a group of special guests, VIPs, coming to the club this evening. I want you on hand to make them feel right at home." Anton glances at his watch. "They should be here shortly."

I smile, unsure who he wants me to entertain. "Of course," I say. "I'll be right out."

He waits by the door, and I close the ledger, pretending not to be as interested in the contents as I truly am. It's not as though I have my phone on me. There's nowhere to hide it in my outfit to snap pictures for the FBI.

But at least glancing at it gave me some intel.

If only I hadn't gotten caught.

Anton brushes past me, opens his desk drawer, and shoves the ledger inside rather abruptly. He holds out his hand for his spare key, snatching it from my grip. "I didn't intend for you to keep it forever," he remarks.

"Right, sorry about that," I say quickly to apologize, not that I mean it. But he doesn't have to know that I'm not sincere.

He locks the drawer and secures the key onto his keyring with the others. Stalking toward the door, he opens it for me, gesturing for me to step out into the darkened hallway.

I exhale a nervous breath. He hasn't shown any indication that he's aware of my betrayal. Maybe I've dodged a bullet this round, but I must be more careful. I can't afford to get caught twice.

Anton laughs under his breath. "Looks like Mikhail is joining us with the ladies," he says.

Mikhail.

He's the head of the Pakhan, the man I'd love to take down and have that accomplishment to boast, but he's also entangled with Madisyn, and they've got a kid together.

Madisyn Carter was previously undercover with the Russian Bratva as Madisyn Taylor. I don't know whether she married Mikhail or not. I haven't been in touch with her since she left the bureau.

But she's the one person who can recognize me and ruin the operation.

We'd been staking the club for months leading up to the undercover operation, and she hadn't come anywhere near the place.

I glimpse her in a gold and black dress, hugging her curves. I'd never known her to wear dresses, maybe a black skirt with her blazer, but she'd always been in FBI attire when I'd seen her. On occasion, back in her bureau days, we'd grab drinks and share a win after a case.

But she has the power to destroy everything and get me killed.

I pull away from Anton. "I have to use the restroom," I say, quick to excuse myself from his grasp as I bolt toward the single-stall restroom and slam the door shut.

I ignore Anton's peculiar glare as I sneak away and leave him on his own.

He says something in response, but it's muffled over the loud music and the thick wooden bathroom door that's shut.

I breathe a sigh of relief.

But I can't hide in here forever or even the entire night. I could fake being sick or, worse, make myself vomit. There's liquid hand soap I could ingest, but that doesn't seem the best course of action.

I just need to avoid Madisyn.

It was always possible that she could show up at the club, but Anton is low level compared to Mikhail. Finding dirt on the Pakhan would make me a legend at the bureau—and a traitor to Madisyn. But she burned that bridge when she got knocked up by Mikhail.

I grimace.

The same could easily happen to me. I've been screwing Anton practically every night, and while I'm on the pill and he's been using a condom, I don't want to think about the implications if I were to get pregnant.

But I'm not Madisyn.

I wouldn't stick around. Anton isn't a good guy. He's not the type of man I want to raise my child.

And that's where we differ.

I can't hide in the bathroom forever. Gradually, I open the heavy wooden door, glancing out, relieved that Anton isn't standing guard. Not that I thought he would. He's probably busy with Mikhail and the ladies who accompanied him.

I glance at Madisyn in the lounge, her back to me, and I sneak past, heading toward the private VIP rooms.

"What are you doing?" Anton's voice reverberates in my ear as he stands behind me. He's taller than I am, and while I've always recognized a height difference, he towers above me, making me feel small.

I spin around to face him. "A client wanted to use the VIP room," I say with a cheeky grin. "I'm meeting him in there."

Anton's eyes tighten. "I thought you were going to help me with the special guests for the evening?"

"As soon as I'm done in the VIP room," I say, hoping I can snag one of the men and convince him to pay for the ultimate experience.

I haven't had the opportunity to use the VIP room, only the booths, which offer even less privacy, although there are cameras everywhere. Privacy is a façade in this place. I wouldn't be surprised if the FBI hacked all the surveillance cameras and watched my every move. Although I'm sure it's for my protection.

Are there cameras in the basement of the club? I haven't been able to sneak downstairs. The key Anton gave me for his office doesn't work on any other doors. I've tried. What's down there?

Anton forces a smile. He's not pleased, but I can't tell if it's because I'm not following his orders or because I'll be entertaining in the VIP room, and while sex can't happen, it's not unheard of for many other things to occur.

I've heard the girls chat in the dressing room. They were swapping stories and experiences, both good and bad, with the male guests. Most girls hate it when it's a couple opting for a room together because, often, the girlfriends tend to get jealous.

Is that what will happen tonight with Mikhail and Madisyn at the club? If Madisyn gets jealous, maybe she'll leave, and I'll be able to work back on the floor where I'm supposed to entertain guests and dance on the platform.

Anton's eyes crinkle, and there's no anger behind the smile. It's genuine. "I won't lie and say that I'm not disappointed. I want you to meet my friends."

"I will," I say, forcing a smile and squeezing his bicep. "When I'm done with the client, I'll find you guys in the lounge."

Anton glances around, satisfied that we're alone in the darkened hallway. He steals a kiss. It's long, hot, and passionate. "Stay out of trouble," he warns.

He has no idea the danger I've thrown myself into and how terrified I am that he will find out the truth. If I can stay away from Madisyn, everything will be fine.

He stalks down the hallway toward the lounge, and I breathe a sigh of relief, sneaking back toward the VIP rooms. I can't just wander in without a client, and the longer I hang out alone, security will grow suspicious and could report to Anton or Nikita that I'm not doing my job.

Fending sick would have been easier. Safer.

But I've never played it safe.

One of the men I've danced for before, a regular, catches sight of me. He's never been shy. He knows what he wants and isn't afraid to ask for it, but usually, he invites any other girl into VIP. I'm sure he prefers the girls he knows, or maybe they just have better moves since they've been dancing a lot longer than I have.

I head toward him to suggest we have a little fun in the VIP room when another gentleman stalks up to me. I swallow nervously as I stare at the older gentleman and offer my most seductive smile.

Supervisory Special Agent Barrett Kingston, my boss at the bureau. He's the one leading the task force. He led Madisyn undercover and assigned her to Mikhail. While Special Agent James Lexington has been my handler, he reports everything to Agent Barrett.

I told James never to return to the club and he heeded my advice. But I didn't expect to run into Barrett.

"How much for a dance?" he asks, pinning me with his stare. The breath is sucked right out of my lungs.

"The VIP Suite is open," I say, needing to save myself from Madisyn and Anton.

His gaze tightens, and he knows me well enough to see that I'm stressed and trying not to show it to him. "Lead the way," he says.

I don't want to dance for him. Everything I do while undercover will be scrutinized. Not that it wasn't already, but I feel his eyes on me and my career circling the drain.

EIGHT

ANTON

Savannah has been acting strange ever since I found her in my office. I run a hand through my hair. I want to loosen my tie—the club is stifling—but I need to look my best.

Mikhail is here, along with the girls.

And the one person I want to show off to them, seems to have gotten cold feet.

Okay, that's probably an overstatement. Savannah is taking on a VIP customer, which is great, but why hadn't she mentioned it to me when I requested that she entertain our special guests for the evening?

I don't want to grow suspicious of her. She's given me no indication that something is amiss until tonight.

What was she doing in my office? I don't believe she has a *thing* for numbers. I've never seen her show any interest in anything math-related.

She was snooping, but I'm not sure why.

Was she trying to see how much the other girls make and are paying the club? I wouldn't put it past her for being curious, but sneaking into my office with the key I gave her was wrong.

The girl ought to be punished. But if I mention it to Nikita or Mikhail, she'll be fired.

No, it needs to be handled by me, off the books, at home, tonight.

I wander into the women's dressing room. The girls are all on stage or entertaining clients. The place is dark and empty. The lights flip on. There's a motion sensor when I step into the space. I head for Savannah's locker. It takes nothing to pick the lock, and I pull it off, opening the compartment.

There isn't much inside. Her purse, some clothes, and a makeup bag. I poke through her belongings, but there's nothing out of the ordinary.

I'm not sure what I'm looking for, but I feel something isn't quite right. Like I've been missing something all along.

The background check came back clear.

I've been to her apartment. I've seen where she lives. What am I missing?

I shove the contents back inside, attempting to make it look untouched. I resecure the lock and head to the security office. I want to verify that Savannah is in the VIP room.

I need to see with my eyes that she's not playing me. But why would she? Does she not want to dance for girls?

Or maybe she doesn't want anyone asking questions about the two of us. I haven't told Mikhail that I've been fucking the new hire, but perhaps she's concerned that she might lose her job if he finds out.

But the ledger.

My stomach tenses, and I can't shake the feeling that something is wrong. I stumbled in, and she excused her behavior like it wasn't any big deal, going through my office.

I hurry into the security office, pull out my phone, and when the camera zooms in on the VIP room, I request them to take a snapshot of her face and send it to me.

There are better pictures of Savannah, but the camera is state-of-the-art, and I upload them to my phone. I don't recognize the client, but we get a lot of different traffic this time of year. It's summer, and it's New York City. We're not in the seedy part of town. We pride ourselves on our establishment.

Stalking out of the security office, I slam into Mikhail.

"Everything okay?" he asks, his arms coming out to steady me, so I don't knock either one of us on our asses.

"Perfect," I say and force a smile. Bile rises in my throat. I'm worried about nothing. I'm sure of it. I haven't been in a relationship since practically forever, and I'm sure Savannah has just gotten under my skin.

I'm not used to being honest with anyone, especially a girl. And while I haven't told her all of my secrets, she's discovered enough recently.

Mikhail nods and doesn't question my word. I head outside into the alley and pull out my phone, dialing Detective Rylan Scott with the NYPD. He's as dirty as they come and on our payroll. He's not a member of the bratva, but he's a trusted ally.

I don't expect him to pick up his phone during hours, but he does.

"This is Rylan," he says. Music in the background begins to fade, like he's taken the call outside someplace.

"Rylan, it's Anton. I need a favor."

He chuckles. "When don't you bratva type need something?"

I don't answer his question. "I'm texting you a photo of a girl. I need to know if you find anything beyond the usual background check that we ran."

"Yeah, of course. How urgent are we talking?" Rylan asks. "I assume you want this done via unofficial channels."

When do we ever want what we're running to be detected? "That's what we pay you for, Rylan."

"Yeah, I'll swing by tonight on my way home and input the parameters into the system. If it pops up anything tonight, I'll let you know. Otherwise, you can expect a call from me tomorrow."

"Great."

"Do you want me to send a copy of anything we find to Mikhail?" Rylan asks. It's not usual for him to get notified, wanting up-to-the-minute information when we're dealing with scumbags.

"That isn't necessary."

Detective Rylan chuckles like he knows I'm asking for a favor beyond the usual request. Probably because I'm calling him well past his working hours. It's nearly eight. The man probably doesn't work a minute past five o'clock. Club Sage is just heating up, and Rylan is likely winding down, someplace scummy with a drink. Thankfully, he's not at the club, which would put a damper on the situation and my mood.

Heading back inside the club, the VIP room door is still shut. With the music blaring, I can't hear a word happening inside the private suite. It's probably for the best.

I swore I'd never been the jealous type. I also vowed not to get involved with any of the girls who work under me. I'm not the least proud that I'm running information on Savannah and hoping that nothing turns up.

Then, I can assume her curiosity is because she's a handful and not playing me.

The doubts keep itching, and I hurry past the VIP area for the lounge, heading behind the bar. I pour myself a whiskey, needing a bit of a bite to handle the rest of the evening with Mikhail and the ladies.

The girls are in the lounge with fruity cocktails on the plush red sofa, watching Violet dance on their table. She's a cute dancer with a great pair of tits and ass, but she's nothing compared to Savannah.

I've got it bad for the new girl.

She's more than just that to me, more than just a fling unless that fling involves crashing at her place every single night.

It's no wonder Nikita is well aware that I'm seeing someone. He's put it together who that someone is, and it's only a matter of time until Mikhail insists on meeting her. I want to show her off on my arm, take her out, and prove to her that I'm not just her boss.

But it's complicated with her weaseling into my office and snooping.

I try to ignore that Savannah is nowhere in sight. I could watch the cameras and see what she is doing, but last I checked, she was in the VIP Room. She'll be there for quite some time; if anything suspicious or improper happens, the security team will deal with it.

"Can I get you ladies anything?" I ask as I approach Mikhail's entourage. He, however, has disappeared out of sight. I'd surmise that he's up in Nikita's office, going over a few business obligations last minute.

"More drinks," Madisyn says, showing me her empty glass.

Lucy begins to stand, and I give her a pointed look to sit back down. She's off the clock tonight and is not responsible for getting drinks for her friends. "Give me your drink orders, and I'll take care of it."

They rattle off girly, sweet drinks, and I head to the bartender, having him prepare the concoctions. Another waitress delivers the drinks while I wander the club, ensuring everything is going according to plan.

Dmitri stands guard near the door. He's not checking IDs. That's Viktor's job.

"How's it going?" I ask, approaching Dmitri.

He stands tall, his back to the wall as he watches the door. "No recent sign of trouble," he says. The Italians and the Colombians shouldn't be aware that Mikhail is at the club tonight, but his presence always puts us on high alert.

"Recent?" I ask.

"One of the cartel's associates came to the door, trying to get in. We turned him away."

"Good." I should relax at his words, but tonight it's not a time to unwind and relax. I'm on the clock, and the Pakhan is on the floor or, at the very least, in the club.

We have our men constantly watching the leaders of the mafia and cartel. It would be foolish not to expect the same of our enemies.

————

The club winds down near closing, and Mikhail has already left with Madisyn. Hannah and Lucy drive back with Nikita while I glance around to ensure the doors are locked and everyone has left.

There's no sign of Savannah. Usually, she's hanging out in my office after closing or in the dressing room if the girls are still changing and packing up.

The lights are off in the dressing room. There's no sign of her anywhere.

Did she leave without so much as a goodbye?

I shouldn't care, but I do. I don't even have her cell phone number on my phone. I could glance at her resume or employment paperwork to grab her number, but I'm not that obsessed.

Maybe I'll swing by her apartment and make sure she made it home.

How did she get home? She doesn't have a car, and I usually give her a ride home. The subway isn't too far, but I hate thinking she walked the streets alone at this hour.

Could she have gone home with her VIP client?

Bile rises in my throat.

No. She wouldn't do that. She's not that desperate for money.

But what if it wasn't about the money? What if she genuinely likes the client?

"You heading out, boss?" Dmitri asks as he pulls out his keys.

"Yeah," I say and stagger near the door. I glance around outside, hoping she's waiting by the vehicle.

She's nowhere in sight. I lock up the club, and Dmitri heads to his SUV, parked two down from mine.

"Looks like you're going home alone," he says.

I clear my throat and give him a pointed stare. "The new girl found herself another ride home," I say. "I've just been taking her to the subway."

"Sure you have. Don't worry, boss. It's none of my business."

"Damn straight," I mutter. I unlock the door and climb into the front seat.

I wait for Dmitri to pull out of the lot before heading toward Savannah's apartment. It's late. I should go home, but I can't stop visiting her and checking up on her. I need to know she's safe and, more importantly, alone.

My blood boils thinking she could have brought the client home with her. My mouth is dry, and I hit the gas harder, flooring it across town and needing to get to her apartment as quickly as possible.

What if she's not home?

Or worse, what if she went home with him?

NINE

SAVANNAH

Earlier in the VIP Room

"I'm pulling you out," Agent Kingston says, insisting I'm off the assignment.

I probably shouldn't have admitted to him that Madisyn is just on the other side of the wall in the lounge. Thankfully, they didn't lay eyes on one another; lucky break, I guess. But that doesn't diminish the immediate situation. The minute I leave the VIP room, I'll be expected to dance for Anton's friends and colleagues.

Madisyn will recognize me, and my cover will be blown.

"You can't pull me out, not yet. He trusts me. I already got a glimpse at the ledger this evening."

"A glimpse?" He raises an eyebrow as he sits on the plush sofa and spreads his arms out on the back.

I sit at the edge of the table across from him and slip out of my shoes. It's against the rules, but I don't think anyone is going to come breaking down the door over a minor slip-up. I stretch my legs and rest my feet on his lap.

"Start rubbing," I say with a wry grin, letting him give my toes a massage.

If anyone is watching the monitors, they can think it's his kink. He chuckles under his breath but rubs my feet, obliging my request. The camera footage will look like two people conversing. The music is loud enough that there is no chance of anyone overhearing our conversation, unlike behind the curtain, where the guards are just a few feet away.

"What's this about the ledger?" Barrett asks. His eyes are trained on me as he works the tension out of my feet.

I almost want to pull away, the gesture far too intimate with my supervisor, but there are worse things I could be doing for him here.

"Anton walked in and caught me reading it," I say.

"Shit," Barrett mutters and exhales a heavy sigh. "We should pull you out."

"What? No, it's fine. If he suspected anything, I'd already be dead." I can't help but worry, and the longer I avoid Anton, the worse his suspicions might get, but there is no chance that I'm going out into the lounge where Madisyn is with her new friends.

"And that doesn't worry you?" Barrett asks.

"Of course, it does, but I've got this. He trusts me. Give me a little longer."

Barrett nods and glances at the camera. He returns his undivided attention to me like I'm his prize. I suppose for the amount he's paying to give me a foot massage, he ought to pretend he's heavily enthralled in what's happening between us.

"Did you get pictures of the ledger?"

"Not possible wearing this little ensemble. Nowhere for me to stash my phone or any other camera."

Barrett doesn't argue because he knows that I'm right. "I'm not letting you out of my sight this evening. When your shift is over, I'm driving you home."

He doesn't know about the arrangement that Anton and I have, that the bratva boss drives me home every night after work. And if I told him, I'd be kicked off the investigation.

Sleeping with Anton wasn't part of the *official* arrangement. I don't regret it, not even the tiniest bit.

"Are you going to pay for the VIP room until closing?" As much as I don't want to be locked in with Barrett for the next couple of hours, I also can't come face-to-face with Madisyn. The other option is faking sick and bailing for the night.

"I have the bureau's credit card," Barrett says with a wry grin.

I chuckle under my breath. "Fine, but I'm not giving you a lap dance." I don't even want to think about what I had to do with James. Barrett is an upstanding guy. He'd never force himself on me. He's practically married, although it's to his job.

———

Barrett's cell phone rings as he drives out of the parking lot of Club Sage. "Kingston," he answers.

The phone is immediately on speakerphone, blasting through the speakers. Barrett doesn't get an ounce of privacy. It seems fitting after the last several hours where we were playing VIP.

"A New York Detective just ran information on the alias Savannah Parker," Dalia says. She's the newest hire, transferred in from another division after Madisyn left the department.

"What did they see?" Barrett asks as he heads away from the club.

"We scrubbed all possible data, and using Savannah's alias, a few articles that we planted popped up, but there's something else—" Dalia says as her voice trails off.

"What is it?" Barrett glances at me and his brow tightens, before returning his attention to the road.

"The detective used a photograph of Savannah to run through the database. It's possible he could be alerted of her status with the bureau if he runs her picture through all channels."

"Dammit!" He slams his fist against the steering wheel and takes a sharp turn at the next intersection. Cursing under his breath, he shakes his head, obviously displeased with this new revelation.

"I'm sure it's fine," I say. At least, I hope it is. I run my fingers over my jeans. My hands are sweaty.

I was quick to get changed and sneak out, being one of the first girls to leave when the club closed.

Agent Kingston heads farther from the apartment I'm renting temporarily for the undercover assignment. "My apartment is that way," I say, pointing in the opposite direction.

"I'm not taking you back to where you're doing undercover work. You're off the job," Barrett says.

"What?" I can't believe that I heard him correctly. He stayed with me until closing in the VIP room and paid for every minute together, only to have me abandon the assignment. It doesn't make sense.

"By morning, Anton will know that you're a federal agent. I'm not risking your life."

Dalia clears her throat. "Sir, if I may—" she begins interrupting him, "it's possible for us to intercept any communication that Anton were to see via text or email. In addition, I've already gone through the main database to block and scrub the detective's ability to view Savannah's information. He could only view her image with her badge number in a broad search."

"Didn't we think of this before going undercover?" I ask, not understanding the situation. The tech team was supposed to remove anything easily identifiable and plant a trail that followed my alias.

"Yes, but we didn't expect the NYPD's involvement with the bratva," Barrett says. "We don't have enough to tie Detective Rylan Scott to anything incriminating, but it's obvious there is a link between him and the Russians."

My head swims, just trying to make sense of it. "Is my cover blown?" I ask. That's all I need to know.

Barrett waits for Dalia to answer the question, wanting her input.

"It's highly unlikely Detective Scott was able to access your file through official channels."

Her words hang in the air. They're as heavy as a lead balloon. "And what about unofficial channels?"

"I scrubbed everything in the database. Social media is a bigger ocean to swim in, but I can assure you that we pulled everything we found on the internet by using a reverse image search," Dalia says.

I want to believe that she's done enough to protect my cover. Years ago, going undercover wasn't as tricky, before social media flourished. Those same tech programs combined with facial recognition software make scanning for an individual's past easier.

I'm honestly surprised the bratva don't have a system of their own and that they're requesting the help of some low-level detective unless Anton isn't contacting his people.

He hasn't come clean to them yet about us sleeping together.

It's not like I've confessed to bedding the man to my superiors. We all have our secrets, and most of us are willing to take them to the grave if need be.

"If Dalia says I'm safe, I trust her."

Barrett shuts his mouth, and I'm sure he's wondering how I can trust the new girl more than the colleague I've worked with most of my career. Easy, I want to stay on this assignment, and she's allowing me to remain undercover.

"I'm advising against it, but I won't pull you out," Barrett says. "But I can't return to the club. You'll have to pass information off to me at a new meeting point."

"It should be Dalia," I say. "You've been to the club. If Anton or any of his men are watching me, they'll recognize you. Just like they did with James."

"Fine," Barrett grumbles. "Is there someplace routine you go once a week that won't raise suspicion? Other than your coffee run?" That's out after the incident with James.

"I grab lunch at a small Chinese restaurant on Wednesdays. We can meet there."

"I'll have it vetted," Dalia says.

We hang up the call with Dalia, and Agent Kingston heads toward the apartment I've been staying in while undercover. It's dark and incredibly late. There's hardly any parking outside.

"Do you want me to walk you in?" he offers, pulling up outside the front of the building.

"I'll be fine." I climb out of the front seat and head through the main doors. I walk up to the fifth floor and pull my keys from my purse when I catch sight of a shadow in the darkness.

It's not just any shadow.

Anton is waiting for me.

I inhale a sharp breath and laugh nervously. "Didn't expect to see you tonight," I say. He doesn't know I'm FBI.

He couldn't know, because if he did, the minute he's inside my apartment with me, it'll be a fight to the death.

"Yeah, neither did I," Anton says. There's no smile. No hint of humor behind his eyes. "Can I come in?"

I get the impression that it's not a question.

"Yeah, of course."

As I fiddle with the doorknob, he's practically at my heels, towering over me. I can't explain the trepidation coursing through every inch of me. My heart pounds wildly against my chest, and my breathing quickens.

I can't let him notice that I'm nervous because if he's not already suspicious, that will raise every red flag imaginable.

"You didn't wait for me tonight," Anton says.

Since the first day I was hired, Anton has driven me home. And almost every night since he's fallen into my bed.

"You mentioned that you had friends visiting the club. I didn't want to impose." It's an easy lie to rattle off as I push the front door open and flip on the lights.

Anton is inside and shuts the door before I have time to spin around and meet his stare.

"I also mentioned that I wanted you to meet them and entertain the ladies. Did you forget?"

I smile and let my shoulders relax. He hasn't pulled a weapon or threatened me. If I look guilty, he'll know something is wrong.

"One of the clients wanted me in the VIP room all night. He was quite the tipper too. I made more tonight than I have any other time." It's not untrue. I forced him to pay me well above the going rate because I had no other customers. The bureau may question the amount spent at the club, but they'll let it slip through because it was all part of the assignment.

Besides, the club gets a portion of my cut, and if I'm not making enough with a single client who has paid for my time all night, it will look suspicious.

"A regular?" Anton asks. His brow furrows.

"I don't believe so," I say. There's no sense in lying. He can see it on the cameras tomorrow if he hasn't already gotten a glance at Kingston while at the club.

Anton locks the door and glances me over. "You must have made quite the impression."

I slip out of my shoes and drop my clutch near the front door. "Isn't that the point?" I smirk and spin around, my fingers tangling in his hair, pulling him close against me.

His breath tickles my neck as he wraps his arms around my waist, keeping me tight against him. "Tell me what you were really doing in my office, *kitten*."

I want to pull away, run and keep a steady distance between us, but that space will only bring about more questions. I don't want to destroy what I've accomplished if Anton trusts me.

"You're right. I was lying to you," I whisper.

He tilts my jaw, his eyes boring into mine. "Tell me the truth." His words are a command, and I exhale a soft breath.

"The girls were talking about what they make each night. How they have to pay the club for dancing, and I didn't believe them when they told me they only paid you ten percent."

"I'll bet Bailey told you that," Anton says.

Bailey does seem to be the most vocal of the bunch, causing as much trouble as possible. Being the new girl, her harassment is generally aimed more at me than anyone else. However, I do wonder who she bothered before I was hired.

"Is it true?" I ask, staring up with wide eyes.

I had heard the girls discussing their salaries and how they couldn't hide any money from the owners. That's why they're not allowed to wear knee-high boots because they pay a portion of their tips to the club.

My percentage was a hell of a lot more than ten percent. Not that it matters, anything I make from dancing goes directly to the bureau. Well, anything that isn't spent while undercover. It's not like I can carry around my credit cards.

"Don't ever lie to me again," Anton says. His hand remains firm on my jaw and gradually is guided lower.

"I swear I won't." The words spill out before I realize the promise that I've made will inevitably be broken.

It shouldn't matter. What we have isn't real, except I don't want it to end. The thought of being pulled off the investigation burns me up inside.

I inhale a sharp breath, expecting him to cut off my air supply, but his hand doesn't fall around my neck. He pulls me closer, crashing his lips over mine, demanding what he wants, but not in words, instead, in actions.

Anton's phone buzzes in his pants pocket. "I should get that," he whispers between kisses. "It's late. Whoever is calling, it has to be important."

He answers the call, putting the phone to his ear. I try not to stare at him and take a few steps backward, gesturing for him to follow me into the bedroom.

Anton stops walking, and there's a flicker behind his gaze, a fire sparked with recognition of betrayal.

"I see," Anton says to the caller. I can't hear what's being said on the opposite end of the line, but the confidence from Dalia about protecting my cover is sinking.

He charges at me, the phone abandoned as he shoves a gun at my forehead. I didn't even see his weapon on his hip or the act of him retrieving it, but I hear the safety click off.

"You're a fucking fed," Anton snarls.

TEN

ANTON

That was the last call I was expecting, Detective Rylan Scott informing me that the girl whose picture I sent over to him is a federal agent.

She's been playing me.

Worse, I thought she had feelings for me, that they were honest and not the least bit wrapped up in her job. Now I understand why she was happy to oblige me, wanting to keep our relationship a secret.

It could have ruined her little game.

"What are you after?" I ask, the gun cocked at her temple. My right hand is on the trigger, and my left is gripped around the back of her neck. She's not going anywhere.

My instincts were right, no matter how much I wanted them to be wrong. When I saw her in my office, examining the ledger, everything seemed to fall apart. I thought I would vomit, but I pushed aside my concerns and swallowed my pride as best I could.

Now it seemed to be biting me in the ass.

"It's not what you think," Savannah whispers, staring at me. Her ruby lips are parted, and each breath comes out breathier.

Is she trying to arouse me to dull my senses? It won't work.

"Try me, Agent Savannah Blakely," I say with disgust. She kept her first name the same, but she'd pretended to be Savannah Parker. Her name isn't the only lie. "This isn't your real home, is it?"

I glance around the barren walls. The fresh coat of paint suddenly makes sense. She moved into this place to go undercover. This isn't her home.

"I'm your mark." The realization dawns on me that I'm nothing more than a means to an end. "Are you trying to take me down or the entire organization I work for?" I jab the gun farther against her temple.

"I never meant to hurt you," Savannah says.

"And you think that I could believe you? After all the lies you've spat," I laugh darkly and pull back like she's burned me. I push her down onto the sofa, forcing her to sit. "Hands on your lap, facing up." I frisk her, and while there's no obvious sign of a weapon, if she's a federal agent, then she's had plenty of hand-to-hand combat training.

She obliges, sitting on the sofa and staring up at me. "Are you going to kill me?" she asks, "because cameras are all over this apartment."

"You're a terrible liar." There's no surveillance or bugs in her apartment. I had one of our guys check the place after she came clean about the FBI agent at the club. Had that all been a lie?

Was he one of her colleagues?

I turn the safety off and lower the gun, but I remain towering above, pacing in front of the sofa. "What information have you given to the feds?" I need to know what she's done.

How much of a mess have I made? Have I implicated Mikhail, Nikita, and the other members of the bratva, or only myself?

"Nothing," she says, staring up at me with those crystal blue eyes.

I ought to pull the trigger, call the clean-up crew, and be done with her. But for some reason, I've lowered the barrel and can't bring it back to her forehead.

"You're lying," I say, stepping closer to the sofa, my knees bumping hers.

"I'm not," Savannah says. "I glimpsed at your ledger but didn't make any copies of what I saw. I couldn't do that to you."

"Because you were caught." Her justification doesn't sit well with me. She doesn't care about me. It's never been about me, other than to use me. Killing her would be easy, and I'm not a forgiving man, but I can't hurt her.

I hate that I care about her.

Her tongue darts out to the corner of her lip before retreating. "Nevertheless, the FBI doesn't have anything on you."

"What about Mikhail and Nikita?" Does she have anything on them?

She shakes her head. "Just my knowledge of the ledger, but it isn't anything that would hold up in court without proof."

I should never have trusted Savannah. Handing over the key to my office had been foolish. I'd made the biggest mistake, trusting her.

"The man tonight, the VIP client, he's a federal agent, isn't he?"

Wordlessly, she nods.

"And you told him about me." I can only assume she divulged everything that happened between us to her colleague or boss.

"Not everything." Her voice is barely above a whisper.

"What do you mean, not everything?" She's avoiding the question. Why?

She presses her lips together, staring up at me. "I didn't divulge that we've been sleeping together."

"And why not?" I press further. "You slept with me, hoping to gain my trust and gather information. Why wouldn't the bureau be proud of that fact?"

"It wasn't like that," Savannah says and stands, skirting away from me, keeping a distance between us.

"Sit back down!" I belt, unsure where she's heading, and I'm not about to let her grab a gun or another weapon she might have hidden away.

"You can't order me around, Anton," she says, folding her arms across her chest.

At least by her stance, she's not going for a weapon. She's defensive. Angry. Like, somehow, I'm the one to blame for her behavior.

"The hell I can't. You work for me, *kitten*. I own you."

She scoffs and glances at me up and down. "In case you've forgotten, the job was a cover. I don't work for the bratva."

I close the distance between us. My fingers grab her hair, pulling her face close to mine. "That's the first mistake you made, believing you can come and go as you please."

I should let her go, tell Nikita that she got another job elsewhere and keep the fact that she was a federal agent a secret. I'm good with keeping things to myself.

But I don't want her to walk away from me or the job.

"Betray the family, and Mikhail will order your death," I say. "But I have another idea." Even suggesting it is dangerous. I don't see another option. "You continue to work for the bratva, and instead of focusing on the bratva, you give them information on the Colombian Cartel. When the time is right, I'll handle Mikhail."

Her brow tightens, and she seems to relax at my suggestion. "How would that work?"

"You're going to offer yourself up to them," I say. "And you take anything that you find while under their roof to the feds."

Her mouth parts at my mere suggestion. "That sounds dangerous."

"It is," I say, refusing to sugarcoat what I'm asking her to do. "If they discover your betrayal and that you're a fed, you're dead. There aren't a lot of other options. You either return to the FBI with nothing, and your work is done. We go our separate ways and never see each other again, or you infiltrate the cartel."

She leans back against the wall. "How do you know that I won't betray you and tell all your secrets to the cartel?"

"I'll kill you myself."

There isn't much that she already knows about the bratva. Of course, having kept our relationship a secret isn't going to let her waltz in through the front gate of the cartel's compound. It would have needed to be public for her to pull it off.

What I'm suggesting is paramount to a suicide mission.

But at least I'm not the one pulling the trigger. Her blood won't be on my hands.

"And your boss? Won't he grow suspicious if one of the dancers suddenly hangs around with the cartel?"

"You let me handle Nikita and Mikhail," I say.

I leave her apartment, my head in a fog. Sleeping with her again is out of the question.

She's the enemy. But what better way to deal with the enemy than use her to achieve my own goals?

Mikhail would be proud, turning another FBI agent from the bureau. However, she hasn't exactly turned her back on her colleagues or her assignment. She's only turned her focus onto the cartel.

I should have just put a bullet in her head.

Any other dancer and I wouldn't have thought twice about it, but Savannah has struck something inside of me. It isn't just the sex, although that is certainly a big part of it. Being around her, it is like I'm floating on air.

Blame it on the honeymoon stage and lust.

Except, sex is off the table now that I know who she is, a traitor to the bratva. And she has one chance to redeem herself and prove her loyalty.

Infiltrate the cartel.

If she doesn't, I'll have little choice but to end her life.

Such a shame.

I stalk down five flights of stairs to my car parked around the corner. I climb into the front seat, but I don't drive anywhere. My focus is on her building and, more specifically, her apartment. The lights are on inside.

I assume she's going to bed, but if she's not, I need to be the first to know. If she sneaks out, I will follow her.

I wait until she shuts off her lights. No one enters or leaves through the front door of the apartment complex.

There's a camera by the back exit, and I've already managed to steal the feed and direct it to my phone.

No sign of Savannah or anyone else.

That's good news. But she could be calling the bureau, and without surveillance and audio equipment inside her apartment, there's no way to know what's being discussed.

Eventually, I head to the compound, sneaking inside just before dawn. The minute my head hits the pillow, I'm out.

———————

A loud, powerful fist pounds at the door, waking my ass.

"What? I'm up," I shout to whoever is at the door. I'm not awake. I'm still in my suit from last night, minus the jacket. My shoes came off, but I didn't bother to undress.

"You look like hell," Nikita says as he steps uninvited into my room. "Late night?"

I don't answer him. The truth is that I don't want to tell him that the new hire, the girl I've been screwing, is a federal agent.

He'll go tattling to Mikhail, and I'll have no choice but to kill her and prove my loyalty to the family.

I should kill her. There shouldn't be a shadow of doubt clouding my judgment that her act of desire is nothing more than betrayal.

But I can't get that girl out of my head.

"What's up?" I ask, avoiding his question. I run a hand through my hair. For Nikita to barrel into my bedroom, something must be wrong.

"I received a call from Detective Rylan Scott this morning." Nikita runs a hand through his hair. He looks rough, even for this hour.

"And?" I hide any hint of guilt that I should have come to Mikhail first and foremost with the knowledge myself.

"You asked him to run information on the new girl. The one you seem to have taken a liking to. Mikhail was busy. Lucky for you, I answered that call."

I clear my throat, waiting for him to continue.

"What the hell were you thinking?" Nikita scolds me, and I'm grateful the door is shut to the bedroom. Hopefully, no one else can overhear his disdain.

"I didn't know who she was. Her background check we did came back clean." It's the truth. I didn't have to fudge her credentials. The feds did that for me.

My options are limited. I kill Nikita and let the secret die with him or face the consequences. Killing a man I've come to accept as my brother wouldn't be easy, but it'd be worse for me to go head-to-head with Mikhail for my mistake.

Nikita exhales loudly through his nose. "We clean this mess up. Just you and me. No one else has to know."

"Kill the girl?" I don't like even suggesting it, but if I don't, he'll never believe I'm still on the bratva's side. And right now, I don't know what I want more: my life or hers. Both of us aren't going to survive.

I'm not a selfless man. I'd burn the world to the ground to get what I wanted. That includes destroying the club if necessary, but that won't save Savannah or me at this point.

"Unless you're in love with her?" Nikita asks.

I don't fall in love, least of all with a vixen who toyed with me to get information. "Let me get dressed."

Within the hour, we're driving up to her apartment complex. Our guns are equipped with silencers to keep the neighbors from calling the police. Although I doubt the situation is going to go down smoothly.

Savannah is FBI. She's not going to go down without a fight.

"Park around the side," I say, pointing at a nearby space around the corner, the opposite side of her apartment. The last thing I want is her noticing we're on our way up.

It's warm outside, stifling, and easy enough to blame my palms sweating on the weather, except for the rock in the pit of my stomach. If there were a better option, I'd suggest another choice.

Kill Nikita.

No.

He hasn't betrayed me. I won't shoot him, even if it means destroying the one person who's made me happy recently.

But it was all a lie. Nothing Savannah said was true. Her desire for me was probably just as much of an act as everything else.

I bite down on my bottom lip, and the pain sensation jolts me back to reality as we head up the stairs.

Five long-ass flights.

It didn't seem long with Savannah at my side. Her wistful smile and laugh made my heart hammer in my chest.

All I feel is pain, bitterness, and emptiness inside. Her betrayal burns me. The darkness will inevitably consume me. Killing Savannah isn't what I desire, but I see no other way out.

I stop in front of her apartment. We don't knock. Nikita pulls out a lock pick and gets the door open in seconds.

I breach the entrance, gun drawn, as I search for any sign of the blonde. There's no sign of her in the living room or kitchen. I search the bedroom while Nikita checks the bathroom.

"She's not here," Nikita says.

I open her closet, making sure that she isn't hiding. The hangers are empty, the closet barren. I yank open the top dresser drawer and then slam it closed, repeating the motion with the next one.

"She cleaned out and left," I say, glancing behind myself at Nikita.

I shouldn't be surprised that she bailed. Convincing her to work for the bratva and worm her way into the cartel for intel was a long shot.

Savannah played me.

She made me think that she would go along with it just to get me out of her apartment long enough for her to pack her bags and leave. Did she go home? Or maybe she fled for a safe house since the bratva knew her identity?

Nikita's jaw is firm, and his eyes tighten. "Did you warn her we were coming?"

I scoff under my breath at his suggestion. "How long have I been out of your sight?"

He folds his arms across his chest, unconvinced, and peers out the window.

"Damn, we just missed her," Nikita says.

I stalk up beside him. She's climbing into a cab. Her luggage must already be loaded into the vehicle.

We'll never make it down five flights of stairs before losing sight of her vehicle if we attempt to follow her.

"We know where she works," Nikita says.

"I'm not going to be able to breach the FBI building with a weapon." He's crazy for even suggesting it.

"No, you'll follow her when she leaves work. Find out where she lives."

I run my hand over my jaw. It's not a bad plan, but there are better ones. "We could just ask Detective Scott for another favor." We're paying the man well for his usefulness to the organization. What's the harm in having him dig a little deeper?

"And he'll likely relay the information to Mikhail," Nikita says, glancing at me. Like the man knows that I can't stop thinking about Savannah.

I'm torn.

I know what needs to be done, but when I'm faced with the decision of pulling the trigger, will I be able to go through with it?

Is that why Nikita insists on accompanying me? He has no relationship with her. He's barely spoken to her. There's no attachment or her clouding his judgment. He'll effortlessly be able to kill her.

I can't say the same.

We head out of her apartment and back into the SUV. Nikita drives us toward the bureau, not that I expect to see Savannah lugging her suitcases inside the building.

There are plenty of people on the street, but no sign of Savannah. For all we know, she could have gone home or to a safe house. Even if we spot her, there are too many witnesses and surveillance cameras surrounding the vicinity.

He circles the block, but there's no sign of Savannah. If she came here, she had a several-minute head start. "Let me out," I say.

Nikita glances at me as he pulls the vehicle over to the side of the road. Cars behind us honk. "What's your plan?"

"Something incredibly brave or stupid," I say and climb out of the vehicle.

He shakes his head as I step onto the sidewalk and lean into the SUV.

"I'm going to turn myself in to the feds." I slam the door shut and head for the main entrance.

Nikita is probably cursing, and I hear the front door slam as he hurries out after me, chasing my ass down. "Mikhail will kill you," Nikita warns. "Think about what you're doing. The betrayal to all of us."

He grabs me by the lapels, trying to make me see things his way. Convince me to come back to the vehicle with him. "You can't do this, Anton."

"I'm in love with her." The words spill out before I even realize what I'm saying.

"Fuck!" Nikita drops his hands to the sides. "Let's go back and talk about this like men. Mikhail will understand. Think about it."

"Because he let Madisyn into his home?" I shake my head, not believing it. "That's different. It's *him*. He's Pakhan. I don't have the same privilege." I won't even have my life if he discovers I knew Savannah was a federal agent and kept it from him.

I glance Nikita over. He looks ruffled, but my stomach is churning like I might be sick at any minute. Does he think that this comes easily to me?

"Get back in the SUV," Nikita says. His face is red. There's rage behind his gaze, and if we weren't in public, he might pull out his gun and threaten me with it.

But he's not about to fuck up his life with Lucy.

"I can't do that." I shrug out of his grasp and stalk around the building toward the front entrance.

Nikita doesn't follow.

The door to the vehicle slams shut, and the tires squeal as he hurries away, leaving me on my own. I didn't expect him to be pleased with my decision, but they'll kill Savannah if I don't do this.

And I can't let that happen.

ELEVEN

SAVANNAH

"A word, Savannah," Agent Barrett Kingston says and gestures for me to get up from my desk and follow him.

I got into work late this morning after packing my belongings from the apartment where I was undercover. The suitcases are shoved into a closet down the hall. I didn't want to show up any later since I'm no longer working on the case.

Anton saw to that when he figured out who I was and that I was undercover.

I stop typing my report, hit the keys to save and stand from my desk, approaching my boss. "Yes, sir?"

"Interesting turn of events," he says somewhat cryptically.

Am I supposed to guess what he's talking about? Is it about me showing up at the office this morning? I knew my cover was at risk with Madisyn coming to the club.

"What's that?" I ask.

"Anton showed up downstairs and turned himself in to the authorities."

He didn't. I gasp and glance behind me. Our interrogation room is empty; I haven't seen anyone else wander inside. "Where is he being held?" I ask.

"Fourth floor."

I roll my lips together. I want to see him. "Is he talking?" Will Anton tell them that he slept with an FBI Agent and figured out I was undercover? That's the one secret I've kept from my supervisors, though it wouldn't surprise me if Kingston or Lexington had suspicions. I made it known that I didn't want cameras in my apartment.

"Says he'll only talk to you."

I take in a sharp breath. The last time we talked, I had a gun to my head. Although he didn't shoot me, he certainly wasn't elated when he discovered the truth.

"And you want me to conduct the interview?" I ask, glancing up at Barrett.

"You know him. You've spent time with him. If he's here to lead us on a wild goose chase, then who better to know if he's playing us."

"You give me a lot of credit, sir." I follow Barrett to the elevator and head down to the fourth floor. More holding cells and interrogation rooms are on this level than any other.

He leads me down the corridor and opens the door, letting me inside the interrogation room. Barrett accompanies me, standing by the door.

Does he think I need protection?

"I want to talk to her alone," Anton says.

He's seated at the metal table. No handcuffs. He's not legally being detained. We don't have any evidence to arrest him. I failed at my mission, but only because he figured out who I was before I could gather anything damning.

"It's fine," I say, assuring Kingston that I can handle Anton alone.

"I'll be right outside," Kingston says. I suspect he's wandering next door to watch through the glass window.

The door clicks shut behind Kingston and locks. I face Anton, not the least bit afraid or threatened by him.

"You got my attention. What is it that you want?" I ask. It's not like Anton to waltz into the FBI and turn himself in. There has to be something that he's planning. I just can't see the bigger picture yet.

"Come, sit." He nods toward the vacant seat opposite the metal table.

I relent, coming to stand on the other side, away from him. I scoot the chair out, and it squeaks against the tile floorboards.

Anton's eyes squint with discomfort, but he tries to hide it. "I came here to save you, *kitten*." His use of the word 'kitten' is soft and quiet, careful not to let anyone else hear his pet name for me.

"I don't need saving."

"But I believe you do. My friends don't like what you did and intend to make their displeasure known."

He's careful not to use words like threaten or kill, but I get the impression they intend to retaliate for my actions.

"I appreciate the heads up, but I can take care of myself." I sit in the chair across from him. The wood chair is cold and hard. It's not the least bit forgiving, and I suspect Anton isn't, either.

Except he's here, and that confuses me.

"Why warn me?" While I appreciate his gesture, he doesn't seem the kind of man intent on protecting a federal agent. He'd sooner kill me than protect me.

He stalls, not answering my question.

"Okay, then answer this, why turn yourself into the feds?" I ask.

He clasps his hands together in front of himself. I imagine he's already been frisked and searched for a weapon upon entering the building. I'm not in immediate danger with him, the two of us alone.

Because, let's face it, we're not alone. Agent Kingston is watching our conversation, listening to us converse, and I'm confident he's not alone in the room next door.

There's not even a hint of privacy, and if I attempt to manipulate any of the equipment, I'll be the next disgraced agent, like Madisyn had been, for what happened between her and Mikhail.

"I told you I'm doing this to protect you," Anton says.

"I find that difficult to believe," I say. "Last night, when you discovered who I worked for, you threatened me at gunpoint."

Anton clears his throat. "I'll admit I was surprised by the revelation that you weren't who I believed you to be."

I can accept that as an answer. It sounds truthful and honest. Not that the man has an astonishing reputation for honesty and ethics.

"And?" I'm waiting for him to elaborate, to say something that makes sense. Why the hell is he here? Does he want to be carted off to prison for the next twenty years?

We have nothing on him or the organization, at least nothing that would be admissible in court.

"I still think you could help take down the cartel," he says and clears his throat, glancing at the dark window where my boss and I'm sure a handful of other agents are standing and watching the interrogation.

Except, he seems to be leading this interrogation, not the other way around. I can't help but wonder what the hell he's doing here. I'm sure the bureau isn't just going to let him go. They'll detain him, legally, for as long as they can—twenty-four hours— and then he'll be a free man.

Unless they can get something out of him.

"That's not why you're here. We both know better," I say and scoot my chair back. If he's not going to talk and provide us with information, I'm leaving.

"Where are you going?"

"I have work to do," I say, pretending not to be the least bit interested in conversing with him. Kingston will be harder on Anton if I leave, and maybe that's what is needed.

When the hell did I become soft? I press my lips together, not wanting to even consider the reason is Anton, that the feelings I pretended to have seeped into me, making me like the man.

I shouldn't like him.

I should despise him, except I don't.

There's a hint of a smile tugging at the corners of his lips. I swear the man can read my mind, but that isn't physically possible. "Sit, let's talk."

"I'll sit if you'll tell me about Mikhail and the operation that he runs."

Anton leans back and folds his arms across his chest. "Why don't you let me do the talking, *kitten*?" This time the pet name slips out, and it's not the least bit quiet.

The room swelters, but I'm sure it's my cheeks burning, not the temperature increasing. I don't want Anton to think that he's in control. I'm the one with the power. Not him.

I approach the door and grab the handle.

Anton groans, realizing I'm about to leave and he'll have to deal with someone else. "Wait," he says and exhales a soft breath of air.

He's gotten my attention. I glance back at him. "Are you going to talk?"

"Isn't that what I've been doing all along?" He gives me a smirk, but there's a hint of nervousness behind his cool demeanor. His exterior is all business, tough and rugged. But there's a flash of anxiety behind his eyes. Is it because he's here and the bratva isn't going to take kindly to traitors?

I approach the table but don't sit. "Tell us everything about the Russian Bratva."

He chuckles and seems to relax. "That could take all night, *kitten*."

"Quit calling me that!" As soon as I snap at him, I regret it. In truth, I like the endearing name that he's given me, but I can't look weak amongst the men at the bureau or appear compromised in any way.

"Yes, would you prefer that I call you Agent Savannah Blakely?" he asks, using my last name, not the phony one I gave him when we first met.

"Tell me about the bratva," I repeat, wanting him to quit stalling.

"You're going to need to be more specific." He's a little too calm and collected for walking in and turning himself in to the feds.

Does he no longer care that he'll be a traitor to his people? "Let's start with the Pakhan, Mikhail."

"Name doesn't ring a bell," Anton says.

"Is there a different leader of the bratva?" I ask. Everything that we've gathered points to Mikhail Barinov running the organization.

"There are multiple bratva organizations across Russia. I don't know any of the members personally."

A loud rap against the window indicates that I should withdraw and discuss amongst the agents. Without another word, I head for the door.

"Savannah," Anton says, wanting my attention.

I'm tempted not to turn around, not to play any more of his games. I open the door and glance back at Anton. "Someone will be with you shortly." I stalk out and shut the door behind myself.

The adjacent door opens, and Agent Kingston steps out along with several other higher-ups.

"We're having him transferred," Kingston says, giving me a heads up.

"To where? Do you have anything to hold him on?"

"We'll find something," Agent Danvers says, giving me a knowing wink. He's another Supervisory Special Agent for a different division. I haven't worked with him often, but there are rumors, none of which are good or bode well for Anton.

I head down the hallway for the elevator. Arguing with a Supervisory Special Agent isn't going to help my career or the situation with Anton.

Just as the doors begin to shut, Barrett slips inside the elevator. "I get it. You're pissed."

"It's not that," I say and fold my arms. "Do you think we should be transferring Anton when we don't even have something to charge him with yet?"

"It's not up to me. But he will talk," Barrett says.

He's a little too confident.

"Are you sure about that?" I press the button for our floor and wait for the elevator to ascend.

"He came here looking for you."

Nothing gets past the man.

"Well, he found me." I shrug and glance up at the display for the floor, wanting the elevator to open already. The small space is constricting, especially with Barrett's stare. At least there isn't anyone else in the elevator with us.

"It's clear Anton's got feelings for you. I just can't tell if you harbor feelings for him."

"I don't," I say a little too quickly. "It was just an assignment, nothing more." My stomach flops at my own words. I can't stop thinking about him being carted away, arrested, and imprisoned. There's no evidence to convict Anton, but I can't help but worry that Agent Danvers will do something to change that. Plant evidence to ensure Anton is convicted.

"Right, even so, you should take the rest of the day off."

"Sir—"

"That's not a suggestion," Barrett says. "Go home."

I don't want to leave, but it's not as though I'm being given much choice. "Fine, I'll grab my things and head out."

The elevator doors open, and I hurry down the hallway to grab my bags. In a matter of minutes, I'm carting my suitcase back to the elevator, and I hit the button, waiting for the doors to open. It takes forever, and once the elevator arrives, I step in and hit the button for the lobby. I'll grab a cab on my way out and head home.

Anton's warning echoes in my mind. But why would he come here to tell me his team will kill me? None of it makes any sense.

It's probably nothing more than a trick to scare me and convince me to trust him. But why would he want me to do that after my betrayal? I pinch the bridge of my nose, my head is beginning to throb, and I'm relieved when I reach the lobby.

I cart my luggage across the floor toward the exit when I breeze past two individuals in suits. They're familiar. I'm sure I've seen them before, but I can't pinpoint where. Here, at the bureau, or someplace else?

Goosebumps cover my arms, and a shiver courses through me as they step into the awaiting elevators.

The doors begin to close, and I gasp when I realize that the clean-shaven men are two Russians, both prominent members of the bratva.

Nikita and Dmitri.

TWELVE

ANTON

"Get up!" One of the agents barks orders at me as he reads me my rights and places me under arrest.

"What are the charges?" I ask as he snaps on the metal handcuffs, securing my wrists behind my back.

He doesn't answer my question.

"I want a lawyer and my one phone call."

The smarmy bastard just smiles at me. "You're being transferred."

"To where?" I ask, and another agent opens the door. Two men stand in the hallway. They're wearing suits and have fake badges attached to their blazers.

One glance and I recognize both men. They work for Mikhail.

Is the agent turning me over working with Mikhail, or is he an imbecile and blindly handing me over, believing that I'll be in federal custody?

I'll take my chances with Mikhail, although I imagine he wants me dead after the shit I did here, showing up, strolling in, and trying to get to Savannah.

I'd be better off in federal custody, arrested, and tossed into a prison cell.

Nikita and Dmitri are barely recognizable. They've shaved their beards, and their hair is trimmed. They both look like clean-cut gentlemen, but looks can be deceiving.

Nikita hands over the transfer papers, and the agent signs them before returning the fake documents. I'm escorted toward the elevator, and the double doors open ahead.

Savannah bolts out from behind the double doors. "They're bratva!" she shouts, raising her gun from its holster at her hip.

I slip from Nikita and Dmitri's grasp, wanting to protect Savannah from the monsters who intend to kill her. She'd almost gotten away.

With my hands secured behind my back, it is difficult to do more than shield her with my body as I rush toward her.

Her eyes widen, but she doesn't shoot me. Is it because I'm unarmed or that she still harbors feelings toward me?

With her attention on me, she fails to notice until it's too late; Dmitri comes at her with a shiv, which he managed to get through the metal detectors.

I have no choice but to knock her backward toward the elevator and attempt to get away from Dmitri and Nikita.

But she probably thinks that I'm working with them.

I'm not.

I betrayed my family to protect *her*.

Agents raise their guns, but no one rushes to Savannah's aid but me. The elevator doors begin to close, and I rush at her, forcing her back into the elevator while Dmitri flanks her blindside and grabs her from behind, sneaking in with us. He lifts the shiv to her chin and slices her enough to let her know he's serious about hurting her.

Nikita jumps into the elevator with us as the double doors are halfway closed. He hits the button for the garage. The elevator descends quickly.

"Leave her alone," I warn Dmitri, but it's not as though I can do much with my hands in metal cuffs at my back.

Does Savannah carry a spare key? If she does, she's a bit busy at the moment to help me.

She knocks Dmitri backward, slamming his body into the elevator wall, and the handrail collides with his lower back. He grunts but doesn't flinch.

Savannah struggles with Dmitri and raises her right arm across her body, turning the gun toward herself. She lifts her arm over her shoulder to shoot Dmitri, but Nikita stops her before she can shoot.

It's two against one.

Not anymore. It'll be two against two.

I ram into Nikita, my head slamming into his chest. Even without my hands, I may not be able to fight my best, but I'll do whatever it takes to help set Savannah free.

The elevator doors open as the struggle continues.

Metal clanks against the floor. Savannah lost her gun, but she hasn't lost the fight.

Boots smack the cement ground from a distance as agents rush down the stairs. Shots are fired haphazardly through the garage.

"Grab the girl, let's go," Dmitri says, shouting orders at Nikita.

Nikita lifts Savannah effortlessly over his shoulder. Without her weapon, she kicks her legs and slams her fists into Nikita's back, but it does little to deter him from rushing her toward the awaiting vehicle.

They yank open the back door of a white van and shove her inside. I'm forced in next, and while I don't want to go, I'm not leaving Savannah alone with the bratva. She's going to need someone to protect her.

The door slams shut behind us, and gunshots blaze through the garage a minute later. Dmitri and Nikita must have had weapons in the front seat.

I shield Savannah with my body, covering her from being hit as bullets ricochet and pelt the van's exterior.

The engine roars to life, and the driver slams on the gas. I didn't see who was behind the wheel, if it was a third member of the bratva or if it was Dmitri or Nikita driving.

The sound of gunshots grows distant as the van speeds out of the parking garage. "We need to get out of here," I say, lifting myself off Savannah.

My leg burns. A bullet grazed my flesh, but it's nothing that I can't survive. I've had worse done to me.

I roll off of Savannah, grimacing from the injury to my leg.

"What's wrong? Were you shot?" Her voice raises an octave.

Neither of us can see in the darkness of the van.

"I'm fine," I say, brushing off her concern. "Just grazed." I don't need her worrying about me. She's the one who needs protection.

"We need to get out of here."

She stumbles in the darkness, tripping over me as the vehicle comes to a rough stop. Her body lands flush against mine, pinning me to the floor.

The rise and fall of her chest matches mine. "Sorry," she says and clears her throat.

"Don't be."

I imagine she's smiling down at me, but I can barely even see her outline in the dark.

"Any chance you have keys to the handcuffs?" I'm optimistic, but it's a long shot.

"No, but there's probably something in the back we can use," she says. She climbs off my body. Already, I miss the warmth and feel of her body above mine.

It'll likely never happen again, the two of us tangled in the sheets.

She shuffles around the back of the van.

Silence.

"Anything?" I ask.

"Nothing useful."

I exhale a heavy breath. "When we get to the compound and the doors open, you need to run."

There's a silence that follows.

"Did you hear me?" I ask.

"What are they planning to do to you?" Savannah's voice is soft and calm.

"Don't worry about me. I can take care of myself."

"The feds aren't going just to let them get away with kidnapping us. They'll follow the van, and if they take us to your boss' home, they'll be waiting for us."

Savannah is right. Nikita and Dmitri ought to realize that, and I'm sure they've already devised a plan. They didn't break into the FBI building and capture me just for sport. "They won't take us back to the compound. They'll drive us someplace remote and kill us."

My first inclination was that they'd throw me in the compound's prison, interrogate and torture me, but Savannah knows how the FBI agents think and behave. They're not going to do a wait-and-see approach when it comes to having one of their agents.

"They weren't planning on you being here, accompanying us," I say. There is no way that was part of the plan.

She sighs softly, and after she makes another round within the back of the van, coming up empty with anything that might help, she slumps down next to me to sit.

"Why did you come to the bureau?" Savannah asks.

Her question catches me off guard. "Like I said, to protect you. Mikhail wants you dead. He may as well have ordered a hit on you because of what you did."

"And you can't convince him that I'm not a bad guy? That I'm on your side?"

I laugh under my breath at her suggestion. "Maybe if I hadn't turned myself into the feds, that might have worked. Nikita discovered your little secret. And when I waltzed into the FBI building, he probably told Mikhail everything."

Savannah curses under her breath. "This isn't good."

"Do you think?" I grimace at my tone. This isn't her fault, well, not all of it. We're both to blame for our actions. "When they open the door, I'll create a diversion, and you run."

"I'm not leaving you alone with them." She's too kind. She'll get us both killed.

"I can take care of myself," I say.

"I'm a trained FBI Agent, so can I."

Arguing with her isn't going to get us anywhere. "Fine." We need a new plan. "Any chance you've got a bobby pin in your hair? Something that I can use to open the lock on the handcuffs?"

"The underwire in my bra has been loose. Don't peek."

I chuckle under my breath. Like I haven't already seen every inch of her naked and shuddering at my touch. "I left my night vision goggles at home."

"Very funny," she mutters. There's a rustling of clothing as I imagine she's removing her bra. I can't see whether she's taken her entire shirt off or done that thing where she manages to pull it via her sleeve. Either way, the image of her perky breasts is a pleasant sight in my mind.

Savannah emits a heavy sigh, and I feel her hands graze mine as she fiddles with the metal wire and the handcuffs at my back.

The vehicle slows as we make an abrupt turn and then jolt around from the bumpiness of whatever back road we're taking.

I'm not sure how long we've been driving, but we're not likely anywhere near the city. They'll want to dump our bodies someplace remote.

Savannah manages to unclasp one metal bracelet and then the other as we slow down again and the vehicle makes a second sharp turn.

"Where the hell are we going?" she asks.

There are no sounds of traffic outside. No vehicles were passing us or honking. We're likely on an isolated road.

"Probably the woods. Someplace remote." There are enough forests outside of New York City that they could be taking us anywhere. The only properties that I'm aware Mikhail owns are in the downtown vicinity.

The handcuffs fall to the ground, and I'm grateful for the reprieve from the metal digging into my flesh. However, it's nothing compared to what the bratva will have planned for us when we stop.

"We need to get out of here," I say and stand, stumbling toward the door. The side door and the back trunk are locked.

"I already tried the door handles," Savannah says. "Any other suggestions?"

The van comes to a dead stop, and I inhale sharply. "You need to run." It's the only way to keep her safe. If I attack Nikita and Dmitri, hopefully, Savannah can get away.

"I already told you I'm not doing that."

The back door is flung open. Dmitri stands with his pistol pointed at us. "Get out," he shouts.

Savannah steps out first. I follow behind her.

Why the hell doesn't she listen to me?

"Walk." We wander about twenty yards before he bellows out his next command. "On your knees!" Dmitri orders.

He mustn't have wanted our blood to stain the outside of the van—too much evidence.

Savannah and I drop down onto our knees.

Dmitri has a gun aimed at Savannah, and Nikita has come around from the side of the van, aiming his weapon at me.

"Any last words?" Nikita asks. "Any declarations of love?"

I'm not sure what he's getting at, but I take the bait. I do love Savannah. I know that I shouldn't. That she's the enemy and wants to destroy the men I work for, but I've already ruined my chance with the organization. They've made that known.

"I'm sorry that it's come down to this," I say, staring at Savannah. "I love you and wish you'd listened to me." Why couldn't she run and save herself?

Her eyes flicker for a moment, and I'm not sure why. Does she have another weapon that she didn't tell me about hidden on her? If she does, now is the time to use it.

"I'm sorry," Savannah whispers. "I never meant to hurt you."

I press my lips against hers, hard and passionate. If it's the last thing I experience, I want to devour her, protect her, save her.

A gunshot erupts, and when I realize I'm not in pain or bleeding any more than before, I expect to find her lifeless body in my arms.

But she's breathing hard, her hands clutched to my hand.

Dmitri falls to the ground.

"Get up!" Nikita barks. "Mikhail's ordered both of your deaths. He won't stop searching for you." He digs into his pocket and shoves a piece of paper at me and the vehicle's keys.

"What's this?"

"Get out of here. Save your girl while you still can," Nikita says.

"What about Mikhail? He'll kill you if he learns of your betrayal."

Nikita hands me his gun. "He won't if you shoot me in the shoulder. I need to make it look like you stole the vehicle and escaped. There's a tracking device on it, though. You need to change vehicles as soon as you can."

I'm aware of the tracker. I grimace and lift the gun, cocking off the safety. I aim and shoot, blasting him in the shoulder.

He curses and grumbles under his breath. "Don't ever come back to New York."

I hurry to the driver's side, and Savannah climbs into the front seat. "You're just going to leave him there?"

"What do you suggest? That I take him to the hospital?" Her question is absurd. We don't go to the hospital, even when our men end up with a bullet in them. There's Steele Concierge Medical and the nurses who live at the compound. One of them is Luka's fiancée.

"Drop him off! He's bleeding out and in the middle of nowhere. He'll bleed to death before help arrives."

"Fuck!" I slam my palm against the steering wheel. Together, we hurry to load his ass into the back of the van. "You're too good of a person," I say, glaring at Savannah.

"And you love me for it."

We hurry out of the woods, my foot heavy on the gas as I drop Nikita off at the nearest hospital. Steele Concierge is out of the way. The bratva will have to deal with the police, which is inevitable after the situation at the FBI building.

We swapped vehicles shortly after dropping his bloody ass off at the hospital, boarding a bus and then a train, heading toward the address Nikita gave us.

"Are you sure that we can trust him?" Savannah asks, glancing at the scrap of paper in my hand with the address, phone number, and name of the man who can help.

"We need new identities. If this guy, Declan, can help us, I see no other choice."

THIRTEEN

SAVANNAH

We constantly have to look over our shoulders. There's no sign of the bratva, but there is an elevated police presence at the bus station and the train station in New York.

We make it to Montana, where Anton purchases a burner phone with cash and calls the number on our arrival, asking for a ride.

Not much else is said over the phone. Was he even expecting us? And if Nikita knows him, how do we know that we can trust him?

"It's okay," Anton says, resting a hand on my arm and sensing my hesitation as we stand outside the train station. "He'll be here in a couple of hours. In the meantime, there's a Walmart not too far down the road. We should pick up a few essentials."

"We can't use our credit cards."

"Yes, I know. We also should get some hair dye and scissors. We need to change our appearances."

It's summer, but today's weather is mild, and I am grateful not to be sweating to death. At least it's not Death Valley.

The scenery is quite beautiful, with mountains surrounding us on every side. I'm used to city life and occasionally visiting suburbia, but I've never been this far west, even for work. "Gosh, it's so quiet out here."

"That's the point," Anton says.

"The FBI isn't going to stop looking for me."

"I take it you weren't expecting this to happen when you signed up to be an FBI Agent."

I smirk at him. "No, this was never even a remote option. Undercover work, yes. But betraying my country, no."

"You're not betraying your country," Anton says. His brow is tight, and he takes my hand as we walk together down the paved road to the store.

"Feels like it," I whisper. "But I promise, you can trust me. I'm not going to contact the FBI and let them know our whereabouts."

"Good," he says and stops walking. His hands begin to pat me down. "Cellphone?" he asks.

"With my purse, back in New York."

He finishes patting me down a little too intimately before releasing his hold. "That's why you didn't offer to pay for your ticket for the train or bus fare. And here I thought you were just expecting me to be chivalrous."

"You, chivalrous?" I laugh. "Don't go pretending to be a hero because of what you did today. Nikita is more of a hero than you."

"Ouch." He lifts his right hand to his chest like I just offended him. There's a wry smile tugging at the corners of his lips. "Why didn't you run?"

"I wouldn't have gotten far. Besides, I'm trained to disarm a threat. I wasn't about to leave your sorry ass behind." I nudge him as we walk. I can't stop thinking about what he said when we were seconds from death.

I love you.

His words play in my head like a broken record, over and over again.

Had he said that to survive? Trying to gain common ground with his coworker and friend, Nikita? Or had he meant it?

"That's the only reason?" Anton smirks. "And here, I thought it was because you wanted to be my hero."

The Walmart is within eyesight, and we stroll across the parking lot. I can't help but scan nearby vehicles, glancing around for any sign of trouble. We're far from New York, but there are plenty of FBI field offices across the country.

How had we managed to slip by unseen at the train station? There was surveillance footage, and while Anton had snagged a baseball cap to cover his face, I was still a target.

"How's your leg?" I ask. On the train and bus, we'd been seated. This is the most we've had to walk recently, and Anton is trying to hide his discomfort.

"It's fine. Don't worry about me," Anton says. The man is tough, but he doesn't have to pretend that he's fine when he's with me.

"Hard not to when you're slowing my ass down," I chide and nudge him again.

"Is that your way of flirting, *kitten*, because it needs a lot of work?"

I roll my eyes and glance down as we step inside the Walmart. There are cameras in the store and, of course, the parking lot. It's not going to be easy to stay out of sight, but if no one is searching for us in Montana, then we're fine.

"Hair dye is this way," I say, pointing toward the right.

Anton grabs a small basket and follows me down the aisle. My hair is naturally blonde, and I have fair skin. I grab the red-haired box because I don't think I could pull off being a brunette.

"Red? Are you trying to get us caught?" He grabs a dark brown color, glances at the box, and then back at me. He probably realizes that my complexion is too fair to have dark hair. He grunts and then grabs the red box, dropping it into the cart.

He's halfway down the aisle when I'm trying to catch up with him as he makes a sharp right and wanders through the razor aisle. "I need to trim my beard."

"Trim or shave off?" I don't want to admit I like his facial hair. Hell, I love everything about the man, and I'm aware that I shouldn't. I'd be safer if I stole a couple of dollars from him and bailed. The FBI can protect me. Right?

Then again, two bratva members managed to waltz onto the fourth floor and capture Anton without incident until I showed up.

"Shave the damn thing off, and I should trim my hair a bit too." He grabs an electric razor from the shelf.

At my insistence, we spend twenty minutes browsing the aisles, picking up a new change of clothes and supplies to clean his wound. After we finish shopping and paying, we go into the family bathroom stall together, and I help him where the bullet grazed his thigh. He could have cleaned it up himself. It doesn't look bad. There's some dried blood, and his pants have a hole from the injury, but the blood isn't noticeable on his clothes because of his black slacks.

We finish in the bathroom and head out, down the road where we've agreed to meet Declan. I don't know anything about the man picking us up, only that Nikita insisted that we could trust him. And he had saved our lives.

Is that enough?

I'm nervous. Not having my service weapon or a backup isn't ideal. But I've come to trust Anton. He's made his intentions clear. Me? I'm still figuring out what it is that I want. I haven't bailed on his ass, though, so maybe I know a little about what I want.

He carries the bags down the road, walking alongside me. Anton walks on the outside of the road, keeping me safe by the grass. Whether it's intentional or not, I can't say.

"Was it true?" I ask, unable to resist the question lingering in my head for far too long.

"Is what true?"

I'm almost afraid to voice the words aloud, fearing that he might laugh or tell me it was just an act to keep us both alive. "That you love me."

Anton keeps one hand on the bags, and his other hand wraps around my waist, pulling me to walk alongside him. "Of course, it's true. I'd never say it if I didn't mean it."

"Even with a gun to your head?" That is precisely what happened. It'd been a spur-of-the-moment, adrenaline-induced scenario.

"I'd repeat it without a gun to my head."

I stop walking and inhale a deep breath. "We barely know anything about one another." What he does know about me was mostly an act. Being an exotic dancer was far from my comfort level. I've had a few wild experiences in my college years but working for Anton, hell, dancing for him on his desk, was the boldest move I've made.

Anton squeezes my hip as we walk alongside the road together. "No time like the present."

———

We're picked up by a dark-haired, tattoo-loving bad boy within the hour. Okay, maybe the bad boy part isn't entirely accurate. He seems far sweeter than any bratva men I'd met.

We drive for a little over an hour before reaching the town of Breckenridge and heading up the mountain to an even more remote part of town.

"Thanks for helping us," I say. I'm situated in the backseat while Anton sits up front with Declan.

"Wasn't much of a choice," Declan says, then laughs. "Family is family, even when you're least expecting it."

My throat goes dry. "You're bratva?"

"Hell no," he huffs, appalled by my question. "My girlfriend, Katie, well, her sister is dating one of the members of the bratva. You may know her; her name is Lucy."

"Lucy is dating Nikita," Anton says as he puts the pieces together. "Small world."

I exhale a heavy breath and pinch the bridge of my nose. Why did Nikita help us? Was it out of loyalty to Anton? Isn't he supposed to be loyal to Mikhail?

I suppose it doesn't matter. Nikita kept us alive.

"Small enough world that he thought sending you here would keep you safe. We'll do what we can while you're here. Get you both new papers and identities."

"That's appreciated," I say.

Declan drives us up the mountain and turns into the parking lot of an automobile repair shop. "We're here." He shuts off the engine and steps out before Anton and I climb out of the vehicle.

I glance around. We're in the middle of nowhere, which is good for hiding but not so great for much else. There's no nightlife around here. Probably not much to do, either.

Anton grabs our bags from Walmart from the trunk and carries them in one hand. He follows behind Declan as they lead the way around the shop. There's a set of creaky wooden stairs that we ascend, and Declan unlocks the front door, handing over the keys to Anton.

"You can stay here until we figure out what to do with the two of you," Declan says.

"Thank you." I step inside the apartment above the repair shop. "You live here?" I ask, not wanting to put him out. I close the door after I enter last and secure the lock.

"I used to live here. It's vacant at the moment," Declan says. "It's a one-bedroom, not huge, but it should do for the time being."

"We'll make it work," Anton says. "Thanks."

Declan grabs the remote and flips on the television, showing Anton how to work the TV and giving us a tour of the apartment. We could probably figure it out on our own, but he's certainly trying to be kind and welcoming.

We're far from home. New Yorkers are always in a rush. I can't remember anyone ever being this hospitable before unless it was absolutely required, and even then, it was lacking. Declan hands us each a cell phone. "Use these to contact me. I've already programmed my number along with my office should you need anything and can't reach me. Where are your old cell phones?"

"Mine's back at work," I say, leaving off the part where it's at the FBI building.

"I left mine back in New York," Anton says.

"Good. You aren't to contact anyone from back home or in your past. You mess up, and you'll bring the bratva to your front door. Is that understood?" Declan seems to be pointing his question at me like I don't know what danger awaits.

"Understood," I say.

I swallow nervously when I glance up at the evening television news report focusing on a segment showing Anton's picture and then mine, detailing the events that occurred back in New York. My stomach churns and I reluctantly glance at Declan.

"You didn't mention you were a federal agent." He runs a hand through his hair. "That complicates things because we work closely with local law enforcement," Declan says.

"Do you want me to turn myself in?" Anton asks.

I'm not sure whether the question is directed at Declan or me.

"No! You turned yourself in to save me, and this is what happened." I gesture at the television, appalled by the accusations about both of us. "That weaselly

Agent Oliver Danvers was out to get you. He arrested you without charging you with a crime and was transferring you out. I wouldn't be surprised if he intended on planting evidence to keep you behind bars."

Declan's eyes widen. "Stay here. I'm going to send one of our team to the grocery store. Write up a list of things you need, and I will bring it to you." He grabs a notepad by the fridge and a pen. "And whatever you do, don't let anyone else inside."

———

"There's only one bed," Anton says as he glances at the bedroom in the apartment.

"That's fine. You can take the sofa."

He smiles and laughs while I write Declan a list of groceries. He asked us to take a picture of the list and text it to him when we are finished. After work, he'll swing by with the groceries and dinner.

"Or we could share the bed." Anton pins me with his stare. "Unless all that passion was just an act?"

My breath catches in my throat. It's not as though we haven't slept together, but that was when he thought I was just a dancer. "Did you mean it earlier, when you said you love me?" I still can't wrap my head around why he said it or why he strode into the FBI Building to warn me that Mikhail wants me dead.

"I can't stop thinking about you, obsessing over you every minute of every hour." He slumps onto the sofa, his arms outstretched on the back of the chair.

I'm tempted to sit next to him, let him comfort me, and fall back into what seems familiar. "I'm told I have that effect on bad boys."

He chuckles and gestures for me to come over. He wants me to sit beside him.

There's only one sofa, no other furniture other than the small dining table to sit at and watch television. The apartment is made for one person, two fit tightly, but it's good enough for us to stay off everyone's radar.

"Do you think of me as a bad boy?"

Is he trying to flirt with me because he's so far past bad that I'm not even sure what he qualifies as anymore? But then again, he did sacrifice his happiness to protect me. He left his family, the bratva, behind for me.

Bad boy doesn't quite seem fitting. Morally grey, perhaps?

"You are one of a kind," I say, and I don't mean it negatively.

Leaving him, would be cruel and leave a giant gaping hole in my heart. Perhaps he's not the only one who has been obsessing lately.

I barely slept the night when Anton discovered the truth about who I work for. I should have packed my belongings and high-tailed it out of the apartment, but instead, I tossed and turned until dawn.

All I could think about was *him*. How I hurt him, betrayed him, and yes, it was my job, but I don't feel the least bit good about what occurred.

I had expected to be elated with taking down the bratva. This wasn't how I envisioned the undercover assignment to go, me fleeing with the enemy, trying to survive.

"You're not so bad yourself, *kitten*," Anton says.

I saunter over to the sofa, sitting down beside him. His hand caresses my neck, his fingers twirling in my blonde hair. We've yet to change our appearances, but I know it's coming.

"We have a few hours until Declan returns. Want to lie down for a couple of hours and unwind? I could put those metal handcuffs on you."

His stare sends my heart racing at all the positions we could explore in that bedroom, just the two of us.

"Too bad I left them in the back of the van," I say. He leans slightly forward. Our lips nearly touch, but he doesn't kiss me. The heat between us sizzles, and I inhale, drinking in his masculine scent. I want to straddle him, run my fingers through his hair, and kiss him hard.

"That's a shame," he says, his gaze never leaving mine. His eyes have darkened, and he shifts just slightly on the sofa. It would be easy to miss. "I do care about you, Savannah."

The way he says my name, sends my insides into overdrive. I'm hot, the room is warm, and I should remind him that we need to be careful. Anyone could have seen us enter the apartment together.

The police could come at any time and tear down the door.

Except, we're in the middle of nowhere, hundreds of miles from New York City.

No one is coming.

It's just the two of us, alone.

And I'm going to have to face the fact that Anton is sitting next to me, and I've yet to kiss him. I want to desire him more than anything, but I'm torn. All along, it's been an act, something that I've done for the job, not for me.

Don't get me wrong. I've thoroughly enjoyed every minute of him naked. I have to accept that whatever happens from this moment forward is entirely because it's what I desire.

That scares me.

Why?

I've never had a serious relationship. I've dated and played the field a little but have never been wildly in love. And the desire building inside of me is something foreign. It's new and unfamiliar. While I chalked it up to the job and my nerves when dancing for him and sleeping with him before, I can't keep lying to myself anymore.

He's not the only one obsessed.

I'm just terrified of the implications. I've left my job at the bureau and am on the run with a criminal.

What have I done? My breathing increases. This time, it's not arousal but fear.

Anton senses something's wrong. His brow knits, and he gently caresses my neck with his hand. "What is it?" he asks.

"This isn't what I signed up for," I whisper, leaning forward with my head in my hands.

"You never thought they'd be the bad guys when you joined the FBI?"

"We have to take down that dirty agent," I say.

"And how are we going to do that?" Anton is wise beyond his years. He's calm and rational as he listens to me speak.

I honestly don't know. If I work with Barrett or anyone else at the bureau, they'll know our location, putting Anton at risk. I can't do that to him, not after he risked his life to save mine.

His hand is soft against my back, soothing.

I exhale a long sigh, and he pulls me against him, embracing me.

"I swear I won't let anything happen to you."

While I appreciate the sentiment, I'm probably better equipped in terms of skills and training to protect him. "I know," I say and offer a weak smile.

"How about we grab that box of hair dye and hair-cutting scissors."

His words are like a ball of lead in the pit of my stomach. If we want to be unrecognizable, there isn't much choice. Especially with our pictures being blasted on the national news outlets.

Anton takes my hand and escorts me to the bathroom. It isn't difficult to find in the small, cozy apartment above the shop. "Color or cut first?" he asks.

I open the box of hair dye and glance the directions over. "Color. My hair has to be dry, and it's better to cut wet hair."

"Do you want my help with coloring your hair?"

"I can handle it. Just make sure I don't miss a spot when I'm done." I strip out of my clothes, leaving on my bra and panties. I prepare the mixture, and Anton's gaze lingers on my body a little longer than anticipated.

"Don't you have stuff to do?" I ask, gesturing at the bag. He still has to shave off his beard.

His top lip twitches. Anton doesn't appear the least bit pleased by my reminder, but he grabs the electric razor and unboxes it, plugging it in to charge the unit. "Needs to charge," he mutters under his breath.

I don't imagine he's disappointed to wait. His gaze returns to me or, more specifically, to my body, as he watches me with the hair dye.

I've slathered on enough dye from root to tip in a few minutes. Thankfully, the plastic gloves keep my hands from being stained red.

"Now what?" he asks.

"We wait. Set a timer," I instruct and give him the information before sitting on the closed toilet lid. The last thing I want is to drag hair color around the apartment and stain Declan's sofa. He was generous enough to let us crash here for the time being. I don't want to ruin his belongings.

"Just wait?" Anton asks, his lips turning upwards into a wry grin.

"What else did you have in mind?" I ask.

"I can think of a few things," he says with a snicker.

"Not happening. If we get his walls coated in red dye, we won't have to worry about the feds or bratva. Declan will kill us."

"You worry too much," Anton says as he stalks closer. "I'll bet we can keep the dye from getting everywhere."

"You've clearly never colored your hair. Do you want to be wearing red dye on your skin?"

He presses his lips together like he hasn't even considered that an option. "If that means you belong to me, I'm okay with that."

"Wasn't the answer I was expecting," I say. "We need the red to look natural. If you go around with red dye all over your hands and—"

He cuts me off. "I could wear gloves."

He's persistent, I'll give him that. "You mean the gloves I trashed?"

"I'm sure there's another pair somewhere around here." He's bent down and fiddling with the cabinet under the sink, poking around.

"You just want to snoop around," I say.

He shuts the cabinet, not finding what he is looking for inside. "If I were snooping, I'd be going through the medicine cabinet. Not a bad idea." He stands and opens the medicine cabinet, glancing through the toiletries.

From my seated position, there's no actual sign of prescription medication, just some antacids and over-the-counter pain relievers.

"Nothing exciting," he mutters.

"You look disappointed."

The timer buzzes on his watch. "Time's up," he says. "Shower time?" The smile grows on his face.

"Yes, but give me a five-minute head start to rinse the dye?"

Anton groans like he's a ticking time bomb and might explode if he can't jump in the shower any sooner with me. "Five minutes? That's a lifetime."

"It's not." I stand and turn on the faucet, get the shower prepped, and ensure the temperature is warm enough.

I strip out of the last remnants of clothes I'm wearing, and Anton whimpers. "See something you like?" I quip over my shoulder at him.

His jaw is hanging open, and while he's seen it all before, it's like he can't get enough. I know the feeling, I want to devour every inch of him too, but one of us has a smidgen of self-control.

"Get in there. You're killing me, *kitten*."

I chuckle and push the curtain aside as I climb into the shower. I tip my head back under the spray and soak my hair, letting the water run until it's clear.

"Five minutes," Anton says, not waiting for me to tell him I'm ready.

He pulls back the curtain and chuckles. "Looks like a massacre in here."

Drops of red dye are on the shower walls and dripping down my body.

"It's not that bad," I counter.

He grabs the shower spray—the showerhead is removable—and douses the walls and then my skin, removing any sign of red dye. "Turn around," he instructs.

I do as he says, turning around, and he continues to soak my hair with the showerhead, letting it drip down my body, and then it swirls down the drain. "I've heard these can make a woman scream," Anton says, holding the showerhead's handle in his hand.

I chuckle at his remark. "Not as loud as you can," I quip and spin around to drop a kiss on his lips.

He reattaches the showerhead before his lips are on mine, his hands encircling my waist, pulling me close and tight against him.

He's barely wet, and I soak him, my damp skin pressed against his. I step back, pulling him under the spray with me. "We both need to get cleaned up," I say.

Dirt and grime slide down his body. We're coated in filth from the woods. He attempts to hide the grimace as the water hits his leg, where a bullet grazed his flesh. The wound isn't deep, but it still likely burns, and the water pounding against his skin isn't going to help his pain.

I grab the bar of soap and lather it in my hands. Anton spins me around, my back pressed against his chest. He pushes my hair to one side, his lips falling against my neck in soft kisses.

"We need to get clean," I say, "before Declan comes back."

"He'll be a few hours. I doubt there's a grocery store anywhere near this place."

I'm not as confident, but I happily oblige, accepting his answer as fact. I'd like for him to be right because that means we have the place to ourselves and each other, to do whatever we want.

His lips crash down against my neck, and from the back of my throat, a deep purr spills out, unintended.

"That's my *kitten*," he says and growls into my ear.

His words send a shiver down my spine, which he undoubtedly notices and is quite pleased with.

"We should finish before the water grows cold," I whimper, trying to retain some small semblance of rational thought.

"We could do that," he says, "or I have a few other ideas that will be far more enjoyable."

"I'll bet you do," I say and spin around, my arms sliding around his neck. "But first, I have to put the special conditioner in my hair."

His nose wrinkles with a laugh. "Are you trying to tell me something?"

"Like what?" I ask and kiss his lips quickly before untangling from his body. I grab the small tube of hair conditioner and slather it onto my hands before running it through my tresses.

"Let me help," he says. His fingers comb through my hair, and my eyes instantly close. His touch is wonderful, gentle yet firm. It's relaxing, especially given what we've recently endured. With Anton, I feel safe and protected.

The water begins to run cold and clear. We finish showering, and both grab a fluffy towel to dry off. I keep the towel wrapped around my torso while Anton's is around his waist. He dresses rather quickly in the new clothes we bought, a pair of jeans and a black t-shirt. I swear I've never seen him look sexier. Well, except when he's naked.

After Anton is dressed, I keep the towel around myself while he carefully trims my hair, shorter, inch by inch. I give him directions, explaining what the hairdresser does back home and how she cuts my hair.

He doesn't want to take too much off, and I can tell he's cautious and methodical.

"Have you done this before?" I ask.

"I don't generally make it a habit of hanging around pretty ladies and cutting their locks, no." A smirk adorns his face as he stands in front of me, checking the length, making sure that my hair is even. "I'm going to have to cut more. You still look too much like you."

That wouldn't be bad if we weren't trying to evade the feds and the bratva. "Go for it. I trust you."

He glances at me, pinning me with his gaze.

I inhale a sharp breath.

Should I trust Anton?

I've put my life in his hands, running across the country, hiding with him in the mountains in Montana. I could have fled, left him, and returned to the FBI.

I'd done nothing wrong. I was taken as a hostage, but now the story on television that we saw made me out to look like I was involved. That I may have had something to do with Anton's break out and the bratva intercepting Anton.

Who had been behind that report? Had that dick agent decided to point the finger at me to protect his career and reputation?

"You look pissed," Anton says. He continues cutting off the additional length, inch by inch, stalking around to ensure that it's even, or nearly even, before opting to go shorter.

"I just keep thinking about that weasel dirtbag," I say.

Anton grins. "You should curse more."

"Are you making fun of my insults?" I glance back at him.

He gestures for me to turn around as he stands behind me. "Quit moving, or you'll get a buzz cut."

"Don't you come near my hair with that thing," I say and point at the counter where the clippers are still plugged in. The red light flashes as it continues to charge.

"Relax."

I try to take his advice, but it's not that easy. When he's finally finished cutting my hair, I hop back in under the shower spray to rinse any extra hair that clings to me.

I spend almost no time in the shower, since the hot water has barely had time to replenish. It's not icy cold, but it will be soon.

I shut off the shower and step out. Anton is trimming his beard at the sink.

"Do you have enough of a charge?"

"We'll find out." He manages to trim his beard to nothing before the electric razor dies and has to be plugged in again.

Anton grumbles.

I bite my lip from telling him that he should have waited longer. He still needs to trim his hair, although I'm not sure how much he plans to take off. It's not like he's got long hair like I did before he cut it back.

I get dressed in a dark pair of jeans and a white shirt with a light floral print. The shirt is cute but not what I'd typically wear. Maybe it better fits my new personality. Will Declan insist on a name change for both of us? I can't imagine that we can continue being Savannah and Anton when it feels like everyone is after us.

I wrap my damp hair in a towel to keep any dye from transferring onto the fresh white shirt. We'll probably owe Declan a few towels, at the very least, in addition to a huge thank you for helping us.

I search around the apartment, find a few cleaning tools in the closet, then sweep up the hair and toss it into a bag in the trash. After Anton is finished, there's more to do, but at least some of it is cleaned up.

When I'm finished, I collapse on the sofa, exhausted.

The electric razor buzzes loudly from the bathroom as Anton trims his hair, trying to change his appearance like I did. When it shuts off, I hear him curse. I try not to laugh. "Out of battery power again?"

The man isn't incredibly patient, waiting for it to charge fully.

He's got half of his head trimmed, and the other half is still full of hair. "Nice look." I try to refrain from laughing.

"It's not going to keep me under the radar," he mutters.

"We're not going anywhere for a while. Let it finish charging." I gesture for him to take a seat on the sofa beside me.

He slumps down on the sofa, brushing against me. I shift around, turning to face him, my fingers running through his hair and teasing along the back of his neck. "I swear if you tell me I look hot like this and to keep my hair this way, I will scream."

I shift my weight forward, my lips grazing his. "I wasn't about to suggest that," I whisper against his lips.

"You were going to suggest something else?" He raises an eyebrow. "Because I could get on board with that." His heated stare makes me shiver, and he pulls me onto his lap. I can feel his erection pressed against his jeans, straining to break free.

"Do you have a thing for redheads?"

"Just one," Anton confesses. "She could be bald, and I'd still want to fuck her."

"Well, let's hope, for both our sakes, that's not in the cards." I grind my hips against his.

Anton groans, and his hands caress my hips, gliding briefly up under my shirt. His touch is warm and methodical. It's both calming and arousing, sending my body into overdrive.

This isn't an assignment anymore. He isn't just a man I'm sleeping with for information. Crossing that line again, it's for me, because it's what I want. He's what I want.

"You've been teasing me all afternoon," Anton says. His face is red, and I can sense his urgency. I feel it, too, needy, desperate, wanting release more than anything.

His fingers caress the tip of my ear, teasing the lobe before his mouth sucks on my neck. I whimper and squirm, my insides heating up from his ministrations. "You like that?" he whispers against my neck.

I mumble incoherently, and my eyelids grow heavy. I'm hot. The apartment is stifling, but I think it has more to do with Anton's presence than the temperature in the room.

He untangles the towel from my hair and lets it smack the floor. He guides my shirt up and over my head. He pinches the back of my bra, unclasping the metal contraption, and slides the straps over my shoulders.

I lift my hips long enough to unbutton my jeans and let them fall to the floor in a heap. "You have too many clothes on," I say, complaining that I'm nearly naked and he's fully clothed.

"You're the sexy one," he whispers against my ear and tugs on the bottom lobe.

I groan, and my insides melt from his words.

"Undress me," Anton commands, and I willingly oblige. My fingers graze his abs as I lift the black t-shirt over and off his head, tossing it behind the sofa onto the floor in the middle of the room. I lift my hips and swing around to one side of him while I help him remove his pants and boxers. "That's a good girl," he says, pleased I've followed his orders.

The way he says *good girl* makes my heart sputter and my insides swoon. My fingers move down toward his cock, and I tease him, making him anxious as he waits for me to touch him.

"I want to feel your mouth wrapped around me," Anton says.

I fall to my knees and take him into my mouth, licking and sucking his shaft.

His fingers tangle in my hair. I listen to his moans and lick and taste every inch of him.

"Good girl," he grunts, and the sounds he makes already have me aching and dripping for him. I don't dare want to admit how aroused I am from sucking his cock. It had always been a chore, not necessarily a desire.

But with Anton, I like watching his face, listening to his sounds, and pleasing the man.

He's struggling, on edge and growing nearer. "Stop." He guides my head away, and I whimper in protest. "Not yet," he says, gasping for air.

My heart is pounding wildly against my chest as I shimmy down my panties and stand completely bare for Anton. I straddle his hips, his cock slick and eager as I straddle him.

I gasp as he fills me, my fingers digging into his shoulder at his size. It's not as though we haven't done this recently, but he still seems to stretch me every time, causing a mix of pain and pleasure.

"Fuck, *kitten*," he grunts into my ear as I begin thrusting. His cock is tight inside my warmth, and I use my hands on his shoulders as leverage as I slowly withdraw before slamming him back inside me.

I swear the man will explode before I do, and he's trying everything like hell to stay in control. "Good fuck?" I ask, although I'm confident that I already know the answer."

"God, yes," he mutters. Anton struggles to keep his eyes open. His lips are parted, and he leans in, crushing my lips against his. "Fuck, yes."

My insides ache with a throbbing building that ripples through me. I clench down onto his cock, my toes curling, and gasp as each new wave of euphoria slams over me like a wave in the ocean.

He bites my lips, and I can't tell if it's intentional or his neediness for release that he's nearly delirious.

I moan and shudder as I struggle to keep my eyes open, staring at him. He's gorgeous, every inch of him. I gasp and moan, not keeping my sounds the least bit quiet. I want him to know that I'm enjoying this with him and how he makes me feel.

"Come for me," he whispers against my ear. He struggles to open his eyes, and his lips crash against mine. His hips rock and thrust against mine, driving me wild. His fingers reach around, stroking my clit in rhythm with each thrust as I slide him in and out of me.

I gasp and moan as fireworks light up the night sky as if it were the Fourth of July. I swear my heart may leap out of my chest, it's beating so hard against my ribcage.

I collapse against him as he grunts and moans, joining me in oblivion.

Panting, I try to catch my breath, sliding off Anton's body as I stretch out on the sofa, resting my legs against him.

He chuckles, and his fingers tease my thighs apart. "Is this a hint?" he asks, his fingers finding my wetness.

"It wasn't," I confess. "But now that you mention it—"

"What's the greatest number of times you've orgasmed in one night?" Anton asks.

"With a partner, two or three," I say.

He grins wildly. "And on your own?"

"I haven't exactly kept track." It's no secret that I have a vibrator. Anton has seen it before.

"The two or three is an easy record to beat. How about I make you come until you can't take it anymore?" He grins with a glint in his eyes. "You tell me when you've had enough."

FOURTEEN

ANTON

Later that evening, after Savannah is sated, I finish shaving my hair and clean up the mess in the bathroom. We get dressed, although she's not interested in wearing anything more than the t-shirt I had on earlier. It looks good on her, although I don't have nearly enough clothes.

There's a firm knock at the door.

I glance through the peephole before unlocking the front entrance.

"It's Declan," I say to Savannah.

She hurries into the bedroom. I presume to put on pants since she's still waltzing around in only my t-shirt. I don't mind, but Declan doesn't need to see her half-naked.

Declan brings us several bags of groceries, takeout, and Chinese food for dinner. My stomach is rumbling.

Savannah returns to the kitchen, wearing a new pair of pajama shorts with hearts all over them. They look adorable, and at the same time, I want to rip them right off her. But we have company.

"There's dinner on the table," Declan says, gesturing for the takeout bag.

I shuffle as much of the groceries into the fridge as I can as he grabs plates and silverware for us, along with two glasses.

"Are you joining us?" He's only pulled out enough dishware for two.

"Not to eat," Declan says. "But I was hoping the three of us could discuss the situation in a little more detail."

"Sure," Savannah says as she pulls the food cartons from the brown paper bag. "What do you want to know?"

"I can get you both new identities. That's the easy part. Is there something else my team or I can do to help you?"

"Your team?" I ask.

Declan clears his throat. "I work for Eagle Tactical. Nikita didn't mention it?" Silence ensues. "Okay, I'm not surprised. We're an organization that helps when it comes to hostage negotiations, private security, rescue missions, that sort of thing. We work closely with the local police department."

He had mentioned that earlier. "Is your relationship with local law enforcement a problem?"

Savannah shoots me a look.

Does she think I'm going to kill the guy? He's helping us. I have no reason to harm him as long as he can keep our identity and location a secret.

"That depends. I need the truth from both of you. What the hell happened back in New York?"

We recant the story in vivid detail to Declan. He sits across from us at the kitchen table while we devour dinner. Neither of us has eaten much all day. Between traveling and our arrival, there weren't a lot of opportunities.

"I'll need to consult the team," Declan says.

"Consult? Why?" Savannah asks. Her brow is knitted, and she looks as confused and concerned as I feel.

"Is that necessary?" I ask. "The fewer people involved, the better."

"I can handle most of the documents, getting you new identities, passports, that sort of thing. But if you want the crooked FBI agent brought to justice, that can't be done in secret."

"Doesn't it have to be, or else we're risking others knowing our location?" Savannah says.

"I meant just me knowing. I trust my team with my life, and you should also."

"I don't know them," I say. Not that I know Declan, but he comes highly recommended to me. The others weren't mentioned.

"Well, I can assure you they have no relationship with your friends at the bratva."

"Former friends," I say. "They want to kill both of us."

"Right," Declan says and nods. "They have resources, but they're tied to big cities. From what we know, places like Chicago and New York. It's unlikely they'll find you in Breckenridge, so long as you follow my instruction and don't use your old cell phone or contact anyone back home."

"And what about that weasel Agent Danvers?" Savannah asks. "He could have ties to your friends or local law enforcement. And while we know he's crooked, we don't know who else might be dirty in the FBI."

"Is there anyone whom you can trust at the FBI?" Declan asks.

I shake my head. "Absolutely not."

Savannah opens her mouth and sighs. "My supervisory agent, he's never shown any sign of being dirty."

"But you don't know that we can trust him. He'll have to report to his superiors if he learns of our location.

If he's as honorable a man as you say, he won't let us remain in hiding."

She sighs and purses her lips together. She knows that I'm right. Savannah may come away unscathed, but I'll be a dead man.

"I can leave," I say. "You keep Savannah here, protect her, and I'll flee. Deal with the Agent Danvers situation, and then we can meet again in the future." Assuming she still wants to be with me after she has the opportunity to snag her job and maybe even further her career.

"No." Her voice cuts all thoughts of fleeing from my mind. "We're doing this together. If I go into the bureau in New York or any other field office, the bratva can just as easily find me. Hell, they might even be expecting me to go and give a statement about Nikita shooting Dmitri."

"Except, the bratva think that I shot Dmitri."

"Even so, the way they've twisted the narrative like we're Bonnie and Clyde, I'm not leaving you behind. And we're not contacting the FBI."

Declan runs a hand through his hair. "Okay. I still have to inform the team I work with about your situation."

"Why?" I put my fork down, no longer hungry. "We trust you because you come highly regarded by Nikita. I don't know your men, and I can't blindly trust them."

"Well, you're going to have to," Declan says. He stands from the kitchen table, clearly frustrated that we didn't just agree to his plans. I'm not sure what he intends to do regarding the situation, but it's clear he's not keeping it between the three of us.

Savannah rests a hand on my arm, trying to reassure me, or maybe she's worried that I'll stop Declan and kill him before he can speak about us to his team. For all I know, he's already mentioned us to them.

"What's the plan?" Savannah asks. "After you tell your team about us?"

"We would work to uncover what we can about this dirty FBI agent. Comb through his finances along with his previous and current cases. There's almost always a paper trail; if given enough resources and time, we can find it. Unfortunately, that isn't something I can do alone."

"Even after we nail Danvers, there's no guarantee it'll clear both of our names," I say.

"We have to try." Savannah stares at me.

"It's not going to make things any better with the bratva." Doesn't she realize that even if she fixes things with her previous employer, she can't just go back to the way things were?

"He's right," Declan says. "We can't stop the bratva from putting a target on both of your heads. But living out here, they won't find you. We'll make sure of it."

I wish I were as confident as Declan regarding the bratva. "Nikita knows our whereabouts, and while he's on our side now, how long will that last?" I don't like sitting around when we can get hunted down at any moment.

"You don't trust your friend?" Declan asks. "Because you came here on his authority."

"Declan is right. Nikita won't sell us out. If he did, he'd be digging his own grave because he shot and killed Dmitri."

I exhale a heavy breath. "I hope you both are right." I'm inclined to get our papers and jet out of town at the next opportunity. But where would we go, and how far can we get? We need help. I don't have access to my finances, and neither does Savannah.

"You'll stay here temporarily. We'll set up surveillance equipment on and around the property, along with an alarm system. I can assure you that you both will be safe," Declan says.

Savannah's shoulders seem to relax, trusting him.

I want to trust Declan, but I've been betrayed before. Not that I think he'd intentionally screw us over. If he wanted to do that, he could have already informed the police or bureau of our whereabouts.

Instead, he brought us dinner and groceries.

The man seems on the right side of the law and honest, which doesn't bode well for me. Not that the feds have an ounce of dirt on me. Savannah swears she gave them nothing, which means anything they've conjured up has to be a lie.

"And what about jobs? We'll need money since we can't access our accounts," I ask.

I suspect that Declan is already thinking ahead, but I still want to ensure everything is planned accordingly and accounted for. It wasn't like I thought that far ahead.

"If you remain in Breckenridge, I'm sure Savannah's skills will be useful to our team. I can't make any promises, but I think we could find some type of opportunity for her." Declan stares at me. "What skills do you have that can help make you an honest living?"

I try not to be offended by his question. "I ran a club back in New York. I handled the books for the club along with payroll."

"I'll bet you did," Declan mutters a little too loudly. "I can ask around. Assuming that you're both staying in town."

"Can we talk about it?" I ask, wanting to discuss it with Savannah a little more thoroughly.

Declan heads for the front door. "Yeah, just let me know what you both decide."

FIFTEEN

SAVANNAH

Six Weeks Later

I've fallen naturally into a routine, starting a few weeks ago with Declan at Eagle Tactical headquarters. Their office is new, freshly painted, and larger than their previous office space.

At least that's according to Ariella, one of the other girls who works for the team. She's friendly and sweet and has been kind enough not to ask any probing questions about my past.

Does she know not to ask or has secrets of her own?

"Savannah, my office," Declan says and gestures for me to come into his office for a word.

The owner of Eagle Tactical, Jaxson Monroe, is already in the office, perched at the edge of the desk. "We have some news," Jaxson says.

He's been running primary on the Danvers case, helping poke holes into the bureau's airtight case against Anton and me.

"Good news?" I ask, hopeful that they've found something incriminating against the man. I step into the office and shut the door behind myself.

"Yes, and no," Jaxson says. "Massive deposits are going into an offshore account with his name, but they're not from illicit originations like we might expect."

"Where are they from?" I ask.

"We're still digging into it, but we have other news on the bratva front," Jaxson says and glances at Declan for him to elaborate.

"We thought it best to monitor all communication among the Russian Bratva in New York," Declan says. "We have audio recordings between Madisyn and Mikhail."

I press my lips together. I know Madisyn. We used to work together at the FBI. "Does Madisyn know about my disappearance and the bratva ordering my murder?"

Inhaling a nervous breath, I'm not sure I'm ready to hear the answer.

"Yes, she's aware, and from what I can tell, she's on your side," Jaxson says. "There's a rift forming within the bratva organization. Mikhail is coming head-to-head with the other members as they question his motives and decisions."

"What are you suggesting?" I ask.

"We can have you make contact with Madisyn. She may be able to run interference with Mikhail and have him stand down. But in doing so, you'd likely have to tell her the truth that Nikita shot and killed Dmitri."

I exhale a heavy breath. "You want me to trade one life for another. There's already been enough bloodshed."

"Talk it over with Anton."

"There aren't any better options? Can't you kidnap Madisyn and bring her to a neutral location for the two of us to talk?" When I say it, it sounds crazy. The bratva will be searching for Madisyn and will kill everyone involved.

"That's not a better option," Declan says.

He's right.

"What do you suggest?" I ask. "Other than throwing the man who saved our lives into the lion's den to be slaughtered?" I'm not about to have Nikita killed to protect us. As it is, we've managed to survive without being found. We'll be ready if we need to get on a plane or another train and get out of town. We have a bag packed just in case things get dicey.

"We can hack the cell phone towers and get you to contact her without being traced. But unless you give her information to prove you're both loyal to the bratva, they won't stop hunting you."

"Loyal to men who ordered Anton dead?" I'm appalled at their suggestion. "I'm not loyal to them."

Jaxson smirks. "It's probably for the best. Honestly, I don't see them as your biggest threat as long as you stay out of the big cities and off their radar. Which leads us back to Agent Danvers," he says with a sigh.

"Anything else on him?" I can't believe, six weeks, and they haven't been able to find more.

"The guy has multiple accolades. He's certainly got the bureau fooled into believing he's a stellar guy," Jaxson says.

"What about Agent Barrett Kingston?" I ask.

"What about him? He comes up clean. You didn't ask us to look into your boss," Declan says. "Is he working with Danvers?"

"No, quite the opposite. Those two don't get along, but if Barrett can't do much—"

"Trust me, he can't," Jaxson says. "Danvers just got offered a promotion. He hasn't yet accepted it, but we intercepted the offer letter."

"Can't you delete it or something?" The man should be fired from the bureau, not given a raise and more responsibility, which likely equates to more agents working under him.

"That wouldn't be very professional," Jaxson says with a smirk. "I wish I could, but even if it disappeared, I'm confident he'll be called into the office and informed of the promotion."

I grumble under my breath. "There's nothing we can do but let him take over the FBI." The room is warm, and I'm getting heated. I fold my arms across my chest. "I don't like our options," I say, "which seem to be little to none."

"There is one other suggestion, but I hate even to bring it up," Jaxson says.

Could it be worse than my suggestion or the one earlier, where we turn in Nikita to Mikhail for our safety? I'd never go along with that, and neither would Anton.

"Well, out with it," I quip, staring at Jaxson. I'm becoming less patient after being around Anton, and my temper is much shorter than it used to be.

"You turn yourself into the FBI."

"Then it's my word against Danvers, and the bureau is already questioning if I'm an accomplice. Besides, that would incriminate Nikita in Dmitri's murder."

"He did shoot Dmitri. Someone should be held accountable for the crime."

"He saved our lives," I say. "We'd be dead if Nikita hadn't pulled the trigger. He's not serving a day in prison for protecting us." The more I'm around Anton, the more I'm sounding and becoming like him.

"Then have Mikhail put behind bars for ordering the hit," Declan says.

"I'm not doing that," I say and expel a heavy sigh. "Anton would never go for it, and to be honest, I get where he's coming from. I'm an FBI Agent, well, I was, and I managed to get inside Mikhail's inner circle. I worked at his club. I slept with one of his men. This is my doing. And Anton would never forgive me if I took down Mikhail, even after the shit we've been through."

"He's a better man than I am," Jaxson says.

"We leave the bratva out of this unless I can safely communicate with Madisyn and it doesn't involve ruining Nikita's life and jeopardizing our own lives again."

Jaxson and Declan exchange a glance. "We'll see what we can do."

There's a heavy silence between them, and I'm not sure what's not being said. "We need to focus on Danvers."

"And we are," Declan assures me. "But it takes time."

"It's been six weeks since we arrived here. That's not enough time?" I thought these guys were the absolute best at their jobs in the world.

"I told you, the money trail is... complicated," Jaxson says.

"What the hell does that mean? You said it wasn't illegal funds, but he's getting some heavy paydays."

"The money flows in from someone higher up in the government."

My stomach falls from his discovery. "Like the director?"

"Higher." Jaxson's expression is grim. "It's political."

"Even so, money aside, Danvers is the one focused on planting evidence and destroying an innocent man's life."

"I wouldn't go that far," Declan says, giving me a pointed look. "Anton is bratva."

"*Was* bratva," I clarify. "And if you can get me a phone call with Madisyn, untraceable, I would like to talk to her." While Declan and Jaxson don't believe it would be enough to get the bratva off our backs, Madisyn and I used to be friends. Maybe I can use that to convince her that we're not the enemy they believe us to be.

"We'll make it happen."

———

Twenty-four hours later, Jaxson informs me that it's time. He provides me with Madisyn's cell phone number and has been tracking her whereabouts to ensure that she's not near Mikhail when I call.

The phone rings, and I wait, holding my breath for her to pick up. She won't recognize the number.

"Hello? Who is this?" Madisyn asks.

I'm relieved that she picked up the phone. "Hi, Madisyn. It's Savannah." I exhale a heavy breath.

"Where are you?"

"I can't tell you that," I say.

There's wind blowing and trees rustling in the background. I imagine she's at a park, probably with her daughter Kira, watching her play.

"You're all over the news. The FBI is searching for you and Anton."

I'd have to be living among the Amish not to know that our faces and information are being broadcasted nationally. "I know," I say. "They're not the only ones hunting us down."

"Well, you shouldn't have gone undercover, Savannah. You knew that's a risk of the job, getting caught. The bratva are dangerous men."

"Mikhail ordered the hit on Anton and me."

Madisyn stalls for a moment. There's silence on the other end of the line, but not complete stillness to make me think the line might be disconnected. She exhales a heavy breath. "It's just business. You betrayed the bratva, and Anton betrayed his men when he covered for you."

"He only knew for a couple of hours. Don't blame him for what I did. That's on me."

"Where are you?" Madisyn asks.

I won't give her my location. I'm inside, seated across from Jaxson. He can hear every word of my end of the conversation. But it's the safest place to ensure that she can't overhear any sounds outside that might alert her to where we are.

"I'm safe," I say. It's all she gets. "You should know that Agent Danvers is framing Anton. Whatever evidence they have, it's not real. Anton didn't betray the bratva."

"The hell he didn't! He walked into the FBI building and turned himself in. I'm sure he wasn't confessing to his crimes. He was asking for a deal and throwing Mikhail into the fire."

"That's not what happened." How can she think that Anton would do that? "You have my word, Madisyn; I was there. He only came to warn me that the bratva was after me."

"I have to go," Madisyn says and clears her throat. "Nikita is coming this way," she warns me.

I bite my bottom lip, refraining from incriminating Nikita in Dmitri's murder.

"Everything that's happened, it's only been to protect me. I love him, Madisyn. You ought to know what that's like. Losing everyone and everything for love."

"I'm sorry, I can't... I have to go."

The line goes dead.

Jaxson glances up at me when I'm finished. "I'm sorry that didn't go according to plan."

"It went perfectly," I say. I wasn't expecting Madisyn to open up to me with welcoming arms. I just wanted her to listen to me, to realize that Anton isn't the monster Mikhail made him out to be. Maybe she can work her charm and help smooth things over. Not that Anton is ready to return to the bratva life, but at least it would be one less organization out to kill us.

———

After a long day at work, I head home. We've moved out of Declan's one-bedroom to a small cabin that we're renting. It's quaint, newly built, but perfect for the two of us.

It is also just across the river, next door to Jaxson Monroe. He's got a top-notch surveillance and alarm system hooked up; if anything happens, he's one of the first to know.

But it's been quiet, tranquil, and almost too perfect. There's a river not too far from the property and a forest surrounding the vicinity.

I never thought I'd like the remoteness, but the thought of the bustling city makes my stomach flop. This has indeed become home.

"How was your day?" Anton asks as I slip out of my shoes and leave my purse and keys by the front door. I lock up the house, making sure that no one uninvited can enter. It's more out of habit than anything else.

There's been no sign of the FBI sniffing around or the bratva, aware of our whereabouts. Although, talking with Madisyn today does make me feel restless. A definite sign of anxiousness.

"Good. I spoke with Madisyn today." I stalk into the kitchen to help with dinner.

Anton is at the counter chopping vegetables on a wood cutting board. He pauses at the mere mention of Madisyn.

"As in Mikhail's Madisyn?" He glances up, unamused by my confession.

"I wanted her to hear our side of what happened, minus Nikita killing Dmitri."

Anton snorts under his breath. "I'll bet that went well."

"Better than I thought. She didn't hang up on me," I say. "And maybe it'll get the ball rolling regarding Mikhail moving on from what happened."

"Hasn't he already?" Anton asks.

"Mikhail not tracking us down, doesn't mean he's forgotten about us. His resources are more limited than even he'd like to admit."

He returns to chopping up the vegetables harder and faster. I watch him, not wanting to interrupt, fearing that he'll slice his finger. I wait until he reaches for another carrot before speaking.

"All that aside, I wanted Madisyn and Mikhail to know Agent Danvers is dirty."

"Why?" Anton asks. "What difference does that make?"

"You don't think the bratva will retaliate when they find out an FBI agent is intentionally planting evidence. They destroyed your reputation. Who's to say that they won't do the same to Mikhail? And they've already infiltrated his organization twice. It won't be another female agent if they do so again."

He pauses momentarily before he continues chopping the carrot. "Point taken."

Our lives have become quite domesticated, living together. "Anyway, I hope that with Mikhail focusing on Agent Danvers, his resources will be thinner, and we will remain untouched."

"Mikhail isn't going to find us out here," Anton says. "You and I both know we're safe."

I hope he's right, but I can't help but worry. "The FBI is still out there, searching for us."

"Yes, but it's been weeks since our pictures have been on the news, and you, *kitten*, look nothing like your photo."

It's a relief how easily we'd been able to mask our appearances and take on new identities with the help of Eagle Tactical.

Anton is now Jason Wilde, and I'm Mia Hawkins.

EPILOGUE PART 1

Anton

Two Weeks Later

I never imagined moving to Montana, let alone a cabin in the woods. Nearly all my life, I'd been part of the bratva, loyal to them as though they were my blood.

But that's changed.

She's changed me. Not that I'd admit it to her.

I love Savannah. I'll always love her. Running away with her, throwing myself on a burning fire to protect her, taught me that she's my only chance at happiness.

True happiness.

But don't ask me to be sentimental. That's not in my nature.

"Are you coming?" Savannah calls out to me. She's waiting outside and pokes her head into the cabin.

We've both agreed that leaving the small town could endanger us. And that's not the life we want, constantly having to look over our shoulders, always on the run.

I'd love to take her to Paris or Florence. Someplace exotic and romantic. But getting on an airplane poses too many risks, even with our new identities.

I won't do it. Not because I'm afraid of getting caught, but because I fear what will happen to Savannah if we show up on Mikhail's radar.

He's been silent, as far as I can tell.

Has he stopped searching for us? I'm not sure. There's been no word that the bratva has left New York, and Savannah keeps me apprised of any news. I'm grateful that the Eagle Tactical guys gave her a job and are helping us maintain a low profile.

I head outside, shutting the door behind myself, and follow Savannah along the dirt path to the backyard, where she's set out a blanket under the clearing of trees.

We could have moved the Adirondack chairs out front of the cabin to the backyard. Tonight, is the Perseid meteor shower, and while I can't take her across the ocean to show her the world, at least I can curl up with her in my arms and stare up at the stars together.

Savannah has laid out a thick blanket covering the grass. Her shoes are off, one at each end of the blanket. I slip my shoes off and do the same, keeping all four ends from moving.

I sit on the blanket, and she climbs between my legs, her back against my chest. Eventually, we'll have to lie down. My neck can't handle staring up for hours in this position. But right now, everything is perfect.

She's perfect.

"Look!" She points up at the night sky as a meteor blazes across the sky. Her excitement reminds me of a child on Christmas morning, full of wonder.

I suppose, having always lived in the city, there wasn't much sky watching at night—too much light pollution. I can't remember when I last lay outside and watched a meteor shower.

We haven't yet seen the Aurora Borealis, but I'm sure that will be another adventure for us to embark on from home. I'm all for exploring our town and our little home.

In winter, there are mountains to ski and snowboard, something I've never done but look forward to exploring. There are plenty of trails in the woods to discover on weekends.

"I have some exciting news for us," I whisper, brushing her hair to one side as my lips graze her bare skin.

"Me, too."

"You go first," I say.

She shakes her head. "You started it. You go first."

"Okay." I chuckle and pull her tighter against me. "On the news this morning, it was reported that there was an explosion in New York City, near the federal building."

She inhales sharply. "Was anyone hurt?"

"A few people."

"And how is that good news?" The smile has disappeared from her face as she turns around to face me.

"Agent Danvers was one of the deceased. He succumbed to his injuries in the hospital about an hour ago."

She presses her lips together. "You and I have a different idea regarding good news." Her brow is tight, and she's troubled about my revelation. I thought she'd be happier, relieved that he can't bother us or hurt her. "Do they have a suspect in custody?"

Her mind must be reeling, wondering if the bratva or, more specifically, Mikhail is behind the attack. "Yes, some low life was sent to prison, and then he got out because his conviction was overturned. It turns out that Agent Danvers planted evidence and arrested him. All of Danvers's cases are being investigated."

"It's too bad that he died and won't have to face the consequences," Savannah says. "I'd have loved to have seen the look on his face when he was caught."

"You and me both," I say. "Hopefully, this will eventually help clear both of our names. But honestly, I don't want to go back to New York. I kind of like it out here."

"Kind of?" She smiles and pulls me to lie down on the blanket. We stare at the night sky, watching as meteors burn across the darkness. It's beautiful.

"You have good news to share?" I ask, changing the subject.

"You're going to be a father."

EPILOGUE PART 2

Mikhail

Betrayal runs through the veins of my family.

Dmitri is dead.

Shot by one of my own, and while it has taken time to come to terms with his actions, it's not entirely his fault.

We are all, in part, to blame. I can thank Madisyn for reminding me that I'd been the one to order the hit on Anton and Savannah. If I hadn't acted so quickly and, in her words, *brashly,* then Dmitri might still be alive.

Anger simmers beneath the surface, like a volcano about to erupt at any moment.

I glance up at the television, the ticker crawling across the bottom of the screen indicating recent events.

We had nothing directly to do with the FBI building being targeted and hit, but I can't say that the news saddens me. A smile grazes my face.

"Ivan, get Madisyn in here," I say. There's a television screen hanging in the corner of my office, mounted to the wall. It's new.

I want to be apprised of all recent events after what transpired with Anton. Seeing his face and that smug FBI agent, Savannah, blasted all over the national news gave me hope.

I don't have to hunt them down. The FBI has the resources to do so and will handle them for me.

And when that happens, I need to be the first to know that Anton is caught. Because, undoubtedly, he will try to convince the feds to give him a deal to save his ass. Isn't that what he was doing in the first place, showing up at the FBI and turning himself in?

Madisyn assured me that wasn't the case, that she had information pertaining to that day. But she wouldn't tell me her source.

Had Savannah or Anton reached out to Madisyn?

I've promoted Ivan after Dmitri's death, giving him more responsibility inside the compound instead of manning the gate at all hours of the night. He's happier, and the young man goes above and beyond, which pleases me immensely.

"Yes, sir." He hurries down the hallway, likely to the playroom where Madisyn is entertaining Kira. It's early, and in a few hours, they'll go out, run some errands to a few places like the park or that 'Mommy and me' class she takes little Kira to.

Madisyn has been an exceptional mother, dedicated to keeping our daughter safe.

"You beckoned?" Madisyn quips. She's got Kira in her arms, and my daughter wiggles out of her mother's grasp, wanting to run toward me.

Kira is incredibly shy, not the least bit like Madisyn or me in that regard, which I find peculiar, but she's not even two yet.

"Have a look," I say and gesture at the television screen. The news is still focused on the explosion that happened a couple of hours ago. There have been a handful of victims, five accounted for who are deceased, twenty injured, and an unknown number still buried in the rubble.

"Please tell me that you didn't have anything to do with that," Madisyn says. Her expression is grim.

"I can assure you that blowing up the New York FBI office was not on my calendar this week."

"Oh, but it was on there for next week?"

"It's a joke," I say, trying to alleviate any tension that may have settled in the room. While I may not be personally responsible for what happened, I'm not completely innocent.

When am I ever innocent?

Regarding the police or feds investigating the matter, my hands are clean. When Madisyn alerted me to what Agent Danvers had done, planting evidence to try to get a conviction for Anton, I knew I had to dig deeper.

If that dirty agent was after one of my men, surely, he had done the same to others who were already behind bars.

With a little investigative work from a friend, I opted to hire a lawyer to represent four men. Each of those men was convicted in cases where the only evidence that was brought before the court was collected from Agent Danvers.

Four men.

All wrongly imprisoned.

One of them was bound to retaliate when he was released.

Can't say I'm surprised. But it's nothing that Madisyn needs to be aware of, or anyone else who wasn't privy to the privileged information.

"I thought you should hear it from me. Do you still have friends there?" While she hasn't been in contact with anyone at the bureau since she left, I suspect there are colleagues whom she still likes and wouldn't want to see hurt.

She rolls her lips together before tugging her bottom lip between her teeth. "Friends is a strong word. Acquaintances, yes."

The FBI burned her when she left, destroying her career because of what transpired between us. It's no wonder she's angry, but she hides her bitterness better than I ever could.

She's calmer, more controlled and collected.

I'd set the place on fire if it solved my problems.

"I wouldn't wish that on anyone," Madisyn says, gesturing at the television screen. "Even my worst enemy."

"Who is?" I'm curious whom she would peg as an enemy. Is she angry with Savannah for what she did, betraying all of us?

"No one at the moment. You have enough enemies for the two of us."

I snort at her remark. She isn't the least bit wrong.

Madisyn gasps as she stares up at the screen. There are brief clips of victims being carted out on stretchers.

"Who is it?" I ask.

"That's Agent Danvers. He's the scum-sucking vermin who works for the FBI."

I recognize the name.

The man is rather bloody, with a gash on his forehead, as two EMTs carry him on a stretcher to an awaiting ambulance. He doesn't appear conscious, but it's hard to tell from a few seconds' clip that we're shown.

"He has a reputation for being dirty," Madisyn says. "Rumor has it that he planted evidence in several cases to get convictions."

I exhale a long breath. "I do recall you mentioning that once before."

"I don't believe Anton is guilty," Madisyn says.

"You don't believe that he murdered Dmitri."

She pulls her bottom lip between her teeth. Silence.

Our family has become tighter, stronger, and more solid, without a weak link like Anton tearing us down.

The bratva life isn't for everyone.

She's convinced me that pursuing Anton and Savannah is a waste of my resources. It's not the financial aspect that I'm worried about but the manpower that puts us open to the cartel. If I have my men run leads across the country every time we suspect that Anton or Savannah might be someplace, there are less men to protect my family.

With the FBI hunting them down, it's unlikely that they've settled down in one place.

And my family is my number one priority.

Which includes the bratva, Madisyn, and my daughter, Kira.

———

Thank you for reading Obsessive Boss! I hope that you enjoyed Anton and Savannah's story. The series continues with **Dangerous Boss**, featuring Dmitri and Sadie's story, releasing later this year.

My sister always warned me not to hike in the forest alone.

Lucky for *him*, I didn't listen to her.

I saved his life, not that he knows who is he, or if he does remember, he's not saying anything.

He won't tell the doctors his name.

There's no identification on him. He's handsome and mysterious, and someone wants him dead.

The bratva believe I'm dead. But the truth is darker and more twisted than anyone imagined.

I'm back.

And while I can't remember the day that I was shot and left for dead by one of my own, I know what I must do...

Sadie won't let me go alone to right this injustice, which means she's tagging along. I suppose that isn't the worst obstacle to overcome. As long as she stays out of the way.

GIVEAWAYS, FREE BOOKS, AND MORE GOODIES

I hope you enjoyed Obsessive Boss and loved Anton and Savannah's story.

Sign up for my Willow Fox newsletter for new release information, sales, freebies, and more goodies.

If you enjoyed Obsessive Boss, please take a moment to leave a review. Reviews help other readers discover my books.

Not sure what to write? That's okay. It doesn't have to be long. You can share how you discovered my book; was it a recommendation by a friend or a book club? Let readers know who your favorite character is or what you'd like to see happen next.

Thank you for reading! I hope you'll consider joining my mailing list for free books, promotions, giveaways, and new release news.

ABOUT THE AUTHOR

Willow Fox has loved writing since she was in high school (many ages ago). Her small town romances are reflective of living in a small town in rural America.

Whether she's writing romance or sitting outside by the bonfire reading a good book, Willow loves the magic of the written word.

She dreams of being swept off her feet and hopes to do that to her readers!

Visit her website at:

https://authorwillowfox.com

Dangerous Boss

Bossy Single Dad Series

Billionaire Grump

Mountain Grump

Bachelor Grump

Ice Dragons Hockey Romance

Faking it with the Billionaire

Daring the Hockey Player

Looking for kinkier books? Try these spicy stories written under the name Allison West.

Boxsets

Academy of Littles

Western Daddies Collection

Obey Daddy Collection

The Alpha Collection

Western Daddies

Her Billionaire Daddy

Her Cowboy Daddy

Her Outlaw Daddy

Her Forbidden Daddy

Standalone Romances

The Victorian Shift

Jailed Little Jade

Prefer a sweeter romance with action and adventure?
Check out these titles under the name Ruth Silver.

Aberrant Series

Love Forbidden

Secrets Forbidden

Magic Forbidden

Escape Forbidden

Refuge Forbidden

Boxsets

Gem Apocalypse

Nightblood

Royal Reaper

Royal Deception

Standalones

Stolen Art